Consumer-isms

In Twelve Easy Steps

Alexandra Kitty

Published by bluechrome publishing 2008

2 4 6 8 10 9 7 5 3 1

Copyright © Alexandra Kitty 2008

First published in Great Britain in 2008 by
bluechrome publishing
PO Box 109,
Portishead, Bristol. BS20 7ZJ

www.bluechrome.co.uk

A CIP catalogue record for this book is available from the British Library.

ISBN 978-1-906061-27-2

Contents

Whatever Happened to the Sunshine Kids?

I

Word up. Yo!
Word up. Yo. Yo.
Word up. Yo. Yo. Yo.

Listen up. Cuz it's the Sunshine Kids!
Listen up. Cuz we got somethin' to say to you.

Feelin' down?
Can't shake your frown?

Let the Sunshine Kids lift you off the ground.

Some days you'll feel bad.
Uh-huh.
Some days you'll feel mad
– Or sad.
Some days you'll feel even had.

But, maties, it's the eighties!
All kids got the power.
Don't let life turn you sad or sour.

Let the Sunshine Kids save the day.

And we're doin' it in the Sunshine way!

Solve it all with a smile.
And you'll be walkin' tall mile after mile.

Don't let your problems get you down. Find a friend or grown
up and let them know how you're feeling. Chances are they'll
know exactly what you're going through and will do everything
that they can do to help you out.

Hey, there! Wasn't that easy?
Hey, there. Wasn't that breezy?

It's doin' it the Sunshine way.
Makin' it another Sunshine day.

Betcha you wish you were that kid.
Betcha you dream to be that kid.
Betcha you wish you were a Sunshine Kid!

Originally broadcast Saturday, September 27, 1986, 9:27 am EST.

II

The opening days of the autumn of 1997 were pleasingly warm and inviting. It was the last Saturday in September and both students and faculty alike were getting adjusted to the cyclical weekday grind and weekend unwinding. The campus pub was never a lonely place on a Saturday night, even at the start of the school year. The large group of tipsy, hyperactive, and eager-to-please frosh had just become acquainted with one another and was competing for various unspoken titles – the Coolest, the Wittiest, the Sexiest, the Toughest, and the Most Mature by sticking with the safest of all barroom conversation topics: childhood television programs.

"Hey, anyone remember the Sunshine Kids?"

"I used to watch that! That little moralizing song and dance thing between the Saturday morning cartoons. It was on all the time, you couldn't miss it, even if you wanted to."

"And they'd all be wearing neon-colored sweatshirts and acid washed jeans, dancing, jumping up and down, and strutting around like they owned the universe, telling us dumb kids how to solve all our problems in thirty seconds or less."

"Perky freaks. Somebody should have pumped them all up with Ritalin. Especially that Kristy. I thought she was going to drop dead from all that psychotic hopping."

"Were they stupid! There was one the segment about how to handle a bully. And I was like real interested 'cause some moron was terrorizing me at school everyday. Then there's Lori chirping, 'The best advice? Be cool, but play it nice.' And the rest of them are nodding like idiots. I thought, 'Uh-huh, try doing that in *my* neighborhood. They'd kick the crap right out of you! Thank you, Sunshine Kids for the cheesy advice. What planet do you jerks live on? Deludo?'"

"But they could sing their propaganda real good. I had their two albums! I remember begging my mom buy all the newsmagazines because they were on the covers."

"I dressed up like a Sunshine Kid for Halloween. Cheapest no-brainer costume in the world."

"I think every talent show in grade school had a group who lip-synched to the Sunshine Kids for their act."

"And got booed off the stage for it."

"It was supposedly so politically correct: there was like twenty kids, ten boys, ten girls; some were little, some were teens, and some were white, some were black, some were Hispanic, and I think there was one Asian boy named Calvin. But, of course, all the white kids got the real face time."

"And there they'd be bouncing around on a white set with that big ugly smiley sun in the background that kind of looked like a disco ball on steroids. And all the big kids danced on the top in the back, and the little ones on the bottom at the front. Totally contrived."

"I know it was awful. But I never missed it. I actually made my parents take me to see them when they were performing at the local mall. I got Plato's autograph!"

"No way!"

"Oh, remember Nyssa? The little one with the huge ass? She'd be shaking her big butt in front of the camera like this..." The young man jumped out of the booth and started to wiggle his

8

backside comically for his laughing companions before he quickly sat down again.

"Yeah, and you'd see her panty lines right in your face. She looked like she had three cracks or something. It was so gross. She danced like a total moron. And she just had that annoying frozen smile that never, *ever* left her stupid pasty skinned face. I just wanted to slap the little bitch silly."

"Oh, come on! You're so mean! She was just a little kid."

"Get off it! Everybody hated that slimy little troll. She looked so full of herself..."

"She was no worse than Jo-Jo; that gangly girl had a weird thing going with her tongue."

"I forgot about that. She looked like a spoiled brat."

"They all did. I couldn't stand Jessica – she had the smugness about her that made me wish her ill."

"Nice! You wished evil on a little girl?"

"An uppity Satan-spawned twerp who needed to be put in her place. Now, Chantal on the other hand, she looked nice enough – even if her dreads flew all over the place."

"Yeah, they seemed to attack Rusty all the time. He always looked so confused – maybe because he was the smallest one..."

"Or just the dumbest. Remember the black kid from Australia? What was his name...?"

"Oh yeah, I know who you mean... I can't remember..."

"Ronald!" one student shouted after a few seconds of deep thought.

"Ronald!" the others repeated brightly in unison while pointing at each other and widening their now slightly glassy eyes.

"Yeah, he was the one who always said, 'But, maties, it's the eighties!' and that was it. Nothing else. What was the point of his pathetic existence, anyway?"

"But he was supposed to be the 'street' one. He was the one who got to wear the snot-green fingerless gloves."

"Hey, dudes, he did something else, too – he was the one who wagged his long skinny finger at the camera."

"And all the Sunshine Kids would be dancing while he was shakin' that finger in the background. It was so corny."

"Shouldn't he have said 'mates,' instead of 'maties'? Did that idiot think he was a pirate?"

"Yeah, but then it wouldn't have rhymed with 'eighties' and you know how anal kiddie shows are with stuff like that. I guess they should have given him an eyepatch and sword..."

"So he could go on a rampage and put all the other Sunshine Kids out of their misery."

"But leave Pitch alone! He was a real hottie. I had a huge crush on him. He was so cute – even if he had that squeaky little voice."

"Heather was a total babe, though. I was so in love with her. How old was she, really? Like twenty-five or something cuz that chick had huge honking breasts that used to bounce up and down – no way was she fourteen!"

"She wasn't *that* old! She just probably had implants or something. She was so creepy – she bleached her hair and got collagen in her lips, I'm sure. She looked like a stoned Barbie doll."

"No! She was my destiny! I had pictures of her and her buoyant boobs on my wall."

"Gabbi was kind of cute, too, but those big bushy eyebrows of hers made her look like Bert from *Sesame Street.*"

"Both of you are totally wrong: Teri was the way better babe. Or was it Jerri? I could never keep the two of them straight."

"For me, it was Correy Corrie all the way – he was so cute and had nice eyes."

"Make me puke! Correy Corrie was a complete putz. And so was Blake – he was the oldest one who gave "the talking advice" in that weird and stiff paternal voice..."

"That kept cracking. It was so strange to be lectured by him. And those pearls of wisdom were so banal and meaningless. 'Don't let your problems get you down.' Gee, I'll try not to, but that big, fat 'F' on my report card means I'm going to be grounded for the next few months while I'm slaving away at summer school!"

"Hey, no one's mentioned Bobby!"

"And let's keep it that way. He was the nothing one, anyway."

"Guys, I know we're slagging them and all, but I used to fantasize about being a Sunshine Kid. I thought they were the coolest kids in the world."

"Me, too – when I was like too young and stupid to know any better. They were everywhere. They did a few prime-time shows, and got interviewed on *Newsmakers*. I remember because I was allowed to stay up late to watch it. They even had their own movie, but by then I was too sick of 'em to see 'em. Lucky kids; they had everything."

"Where are they now? I mean, besides the dead one, and Griffen; that guy is everywhere."

"Didn't one of them get busted for drugs?"

"Think so. I don't know about the rest of 'em, though."

"Probably living off royalties and never having to work again. Either that or doing that dance at a Vegas cathouse!"

"And singing that stupid song –"

On cue, the frosh broke out in drunken unison, "Betcha you wish you were that kid! Betcha you dream to be that kid! Betcha you wish you were a Sunshine Kid!"

III
Thursday, September 27, 2007

9 p.m. *(38)* ****1/2 Retrodocs:** *Whatever Happened to the Sunshine Kids?* *(2006): This documentary looks at the adult lives of the '80's preteen pop culture phenomena The Sunshine Kids 20 years after their television debut. Includes interviews with the former child stars of the series and original footage.* (R) (CC)

IV

BOBBY: Everything about the Sunshine Kids was illogical, but it was illogical in all the right ways at the time: for kids who pretended they didn't need grownups to think up all the answers to life's problems, we certainly always told kids to ask their parents or teachers to solve their problems for them. Those segments must have been the most elaborate way of saying, "Ask your mom and dad!" imaginable. The show was to make the audience think that they were also "Sunshine Kids" who hung out with us, but that got lost in translation. The producers dressed us in neon tops to make us seem like regular kids, but all it did was isolate us from our peers. At first kids admired us and wanted to be us, by the end of the second season, they wanted to stomp us into the ground. For a show that preached about empowering children, it did anything but empower the twenty children who worked on it.

*

GABBI: Well, of course, we never had "all the answers" for every problem in the world – we were just kids reading scripts and doing what we were told. (laughs) It's not like we really had a clue about life. I know I didn't. If I did, I wouldn't have dropped out of school at fifteen. Or gotten hooked on meth. Or find myself living in a woman's shelter after finding my live-in boyfriend messing with my son.

*

KRISTY: Well, the original sign off wasn't "Betcha you wish you were a Sunshine Kid!" There was another spoken line tagged on at the end where Blake said, "Well, you can be!" But when the first one aired, there was a glitch with the audio and it got cut off. Who would've thought all the TV critics would have nothing better to do than to write about us and praise our...what did the guy from the *Post* call it –? Our "cool, spunky tyke-a-tude?" So after that, the producers just dropped the last line because they thought it was great. They didn't think that as we got more famous, a lot of kids would begin to resent that line. It

made us look like know-it-all snobs.
*

JESSICA: That last line brought us fame, and then it brought us infamy. It really turned on us. I remember moms would stop me on the street and praise me for that, and then suddenly, moms would stop me on the street to yell at me and call me a stuck-up little you-know-what who thought that I was better than her kids. It really, really hurt. I couldn't understand it. I was doing everything I was told and doing everything the same way, but one day I was a good person, and the next I was a bad person. I used to cry in my room all day long for months.
*

NYSSA: Oh, my god, there was no end to infighting among our parents back then. Heather's mom thought her daughter was the Queen Bee and was a total control-freak diva on the set. She terrorized the other girls and used to have Jerri and Teri in tears – she did that so their eyes would look puffier and they wouldn't look as good as Heather. She made Heather dye her hair and get implants. Where's Child Welfare Services when you need them? And we needed them, right there on the set. And I don't want to mention Griffen's parents. They always made sure he got the most face time and was positioned the best. They obsessed over lighting and camera angles and which lines he would get. They made sure he would say, "All kids have the power" because they wanted him to appear confident, but they didn't want him to be on camera when we started with that humiliating "Word up, yo" ditty at the beginning because they didn't want him to be associated with that stupidity. Which just goes to show any pair of psychopathic control freaks with evil genes are allowed to reproduce – but at least they had a point. (laughs) God, that song was awful.
*

JESSICA: We never really got along on the set; so I guess most of us never really kept in contact with each other, though I'm sure we all kind of kept tabs on each other through the media –

first because of a little professional jealousy – which ones would go on to become the "big stars," but when it became clear most of us weren't going to have that real big break, the keeping tabs became a lot more sinister – which one of us was going to get into trouble now? Then it got worse when Rusty killed himself in his car, and then Benet joined a gang and got gunned down during a shootout: which Sunshine Kid was the next to die? Nyssa came close so many times over the years it wasn't funny, but then Plato got drunk and got himself killed in a car accident; so he wasn't going to rise from the ashes like Nyssa always does. Then it was girls' turn to meet untimely demises: Lori overdosed; Chantal got beaten to death by her boyfriend; Jo-Jo was always so sickly that you knew she'd go young; and who knows if Heather killed herself, overdosed, or was murdered? You just sort of cringe when the next body turns up at a morgue, and pray that it's not you who's next. That's why I left the business and rediscovered my spirituality. I am proud to say I am a stay-at-home mom, home-schooling my seven children. Even though money is extremely tight with us, I still manage to instill proper discipline into all of my children.

INTERVIEWER: Does any one tragedy stand out to you?

JESSICA: Griffen's downfall was a real shocker to me. I thought he'd do the best of us all, and he got so painfully close. So very, very close. Even though I never liked him or got along with him, I was really hoping he would do it to vindicate the Sunshine Kids' sullied name – he had the momentum, support and presence to pull it all off – but then ... then, he just, just lost it all; so very quickly. It pains me to think about it to this day. The news was worse than even Jo-Jo's passing. And it's hard to trump an early death by terminal illness.
*
NYSSA: The Former Child Performer's Lobby? Oh, please. A bunch of image-spinning fascists. Go against 'em and tell the

truth about what happens to discarded B-list child stars and they go after you. "We're saddened and disappointed that Nyssa has chosen to publicly disparage us with slander and unfounded innuendo while refusing to take responsibility for her own actions, which represent the minority of former child performers." Funny they're never saddened that "the business" sucked me dry. Hey – I was lying in the hospital alone, broke, beaten, addicted, and almost dying of anorexia, and they did everything they could to keep it quiet so that the news of my eating disorder and heroin addiction wouldn't overshadow Griffen's movie debut. And that movie blew worse chunks than I ever did, by the way. (laughs)

*

TERI: Of all of us, Griffen and Heather had the most on-set support. Heather because she had the uber stage mother who tried to make it The Heather Show, and Griffen because the producers saw something in him that they didn't see in us, but his parents were always on the set, too. When we were interviewed on *Newsmakers*, Griffen did almost all of the talking, which was the first sign that there were bigger plans for him. I thought it would be Blake who'd answer the most questions because he was the oldest and the de facto "star" of those shorts. The TV specials were more about Heather, but Griffen stole every scene – something he was very good at, even better than Corrie. By the time the movie came out, it was Griffen's vehicle all the way.

*

KRISTY: Was I resentful? Yes, of course I was, although I doubt I was as bitter as Nyssa. The producers didn't keep in contact with any of the kids but Griffen. When we filmed our last short, the producers said "Good-bye" to all of us, but said, "We'll see you next week" to Griffen. The following year, he was a supporting character on a sitcom, playing a sarcastic teen to an upwardly mobile family. The show bombed, but then Griffen was on another show, this time as the lead. Then his solo album came out. Then he got a role in a movie. It didn't do very well, but Griffen kept showing up in bigger roles, always getting the buzz and attention. Then he got his big break, and became a heartthrob.

INTERVIEWER: Where were you when all this was happening?

KRISTY: Getting stoned and horny with the various boyfriends and johns I had, but I think everybody already knew that with that tape coming out and all...
*

JERRI: Money? We didn't get paid very much at all. You have to remember we didn't have an actual show – it was just filler between the real shows. For our TV specials and movie, we were paid SAG scale, meaning we didn't get a whole lot of money. The albums and mall tour were also done on a shoestring budget. I didn't realize how little I was paid at the time. When I turned eighteen, I got my money out of trust and I almost fell over how little I actually got. I burned through that money like nothing.
*

BOBBY: I wish I could shake the name "Bobby," but I've given up on that a long time ago. (laughs) It's Roberto, but you know what they say about first impressions – they're the ones that last forever. That's the hardest thing, most people first saw me when I was seven, and in their minds I'm always that little boy dancing at the front of a stage. I never got to say much, even during the prime-time shows or the movie. I was one of the generic kids, -- the filler who smiled and looked cute on cue. That's hardly being a role model for my people, but I thought I was doing something positive and important back then. I could never imagine how wrong I was. I gave up on being the positive role model when the show ended and just drifted for the next twenty years.
*

RONALD: We were big for about tens seconds – really big ... at least what a thirteen year old thought was big – and then it just crashed. Boom. Poof. Gone. In two years we did the gazillion segments, three prime-time specials, that mall tour, two albums, and then that stinker of a movie, and then ... nothing. The fan mail stopped. The calls stopped. The coverage stopped. And there was nothing to replace it with. No one wanted to hire a Sunshine Kid, except for Griffen for a while, and now he's even more tainted than the rest of us. It nearly killed me. I know it killed Plato and Benet. It really did. Ben was always a joiner. He always had to run with a crowd, any crowd; so long as they'd take him. I'm sure that gang who took him set him up just so they could dispose of him for kicks. Plato got restless and angry. He was driving like a maniac when his car crashed. Me, I just had no idea who I was and where I wanted to be. No, that's a lie. I knew what I wanted to be, but I wasn't allowed to be it. It was a losing battle and hated what I was forced to be. So I re-belled. And lost.

*

TERI: I got lost in the crowd, and it didn't help that Jerri's name rhymed with mine. No one could ever keep the two of us straight so we canceled each other out. We sort of blended in and became one person in everybody's mind; so I thought my slate would be clear once production stopped – I would have some acting experience under my belt but would still be anony-mous enough to get some decent roles. It never happened, and I became depressed. First I was the nobody on a popular little non-show, and then I was just a nobody.

*

BLAKE: Yeah, I was into drugs, just like the rest of them. One of the assistants on the set was a dealer; so most of the older kids got hooked on speed on the show. That's why so many of us were jumping off the walls. They used to call us the "junior junk-ies." The army changed my life. I mean, I was given a discharge, but at least it straightened me out enough to gain employment as a mechanic. Some of us weren't as lucky. Look at Corrie. He kind of always used his charms and looks to get special treatment on the set, and it didn't surprise me one bit when I heard he started to use his body to get his way after our movie bombed. Except it backfired and he became a D-list porn star who played both sides of the fence. Thanks to him, the phrase "doing it the Sunshine way" took on a whole new meaning. (laughs) Which is really too bad since despite everything, we were trying to get across a positive message for young people – not to give up and do the right thing. I know I try to live by that still, even though it's not always easy.

*

CORRIE CORREY: I don't know if you could say I chose to become a porn star, but I wanted to make a comeback in the entertainment business, and it was the only option available to me at the time. But I've left that business and am trying to put that – and my Sunshine days behind me. And please, no jokes about the last remark. That's all I have to say about both.

*

RONALD: It's ridiculous, really. I've served out most of my sentence for the armed robbery, and I am going to be released from this place next year, but when I get out, I know I'll be put in another jail – people go up to me and say, "Hey, *matie*, didn't you used to be Ronald?" It's crazy; I'm still Ronald, but they won't let me be Ronald. I haven't been a Sunshine Kid in how many years, and they won't let me be anything else but that. Prison's different now, I'm allowed to be Ronald. No one talks about the Sunshine stuff, anymore. So I guess in a way prison's a freer place than the outside world. (laughs) Ronald can be Ronald in jail and nowhere else.

*

JERRI: The first time I was caught for writing bad checks I was twenty-three. Then I was busted for shoplifting a year later. Bad checks again two months later. Then I was caught using a stolen credit card twice, no, three times after that. You know, I've never really stolen big, I just tried to cover my rent and insurance. I dropped out of school young, and I haven't had any great jobs in my life, and living costs money. No one wants to hire an uneducated carnival freak. It's hard to be a has-been at thirteen. It's over before it even began. I never could possibly dream in my worst nightmare, that at thirty-one I'd be broke and in prison. A single mother who had to leave her three kids in a foster home... (cries)

*

KRISTY: No, I never really hung out with Chantal; no one did. Or Rusty. They were kind of loners. Looking back, I think Griffen kind of set the tone for that. He picked on those two, so they withdrew. He used to call Rusty "Runty" and the name stuck on the set. And if I remember it right, he called Stevie "Pitch" on the first day, and the producers thought it was a catchy nickname; so that's what they used. Griffen didn't call Chantal any name in particular; he used to make all sorts of negative comments about her looks and performance. I could tell it hurt her deeply, but nobody wanted to do anything about it because Griffen had all the power – he was the producers' favorite and he used it to his advantage. Lori once tried to stand up for Chantal, but then she was practically written out of the show. That's the kind of pull Griffen and his parents had.

*

NYSSA: For years, I used to think I was the fattest and ugliest little kid on the planet with the ugliest smile. I couldn't even look at reruns or old pictures of myself. Then, last year, I got out of rehab – my little home away from home (laughs) – and made myself look at the old episodes and the photos. And you know what? I wasn't fat at all – I just was a little fuller than the other girls who were all underweight. I was a pretty cute kid! I was so mad that I wanted to go out and break some kneecaps, but then I remembered that would have violated the terms of my probation. (laughs) I guess I was just the turd everyone wanted to hate – and Griffen was the turd everyone wanted to love.

*

BLAKE: Poor Jo-Jo. She was such a trooper; she had her share of health problems – a weak heart, diabetes, asthma, chronic pain, you name it, and yet she was a professional and team player from beginning to end. The hot lights were the worst for her, though. She would be so faint from all that heat and dancing that she couldn't always keep her tongue in her mouth, but she always did everything with a smile and a kind word. Her mother would bully her into working, even when she was in a lot of pain. "A leading lady never quits!" her mom would keep saying. The directors weren't any better. Jo-Jo should have never been forced to work ... all that strenuous dancing, rehearsing, and touring just weakened her body. I wish I went to her funeral five years ago, but I was too selfish then. I didn't want to be associated with the Sunshine Kids anymore; so I thought going there would just stick that Sunshine label on me again. It's a regret; she never complained, and she deserved better than what she got. Of all of us, she was the only one who truly deserved to be called a Sunshine Kid.

*

CALVIN: Yes, I am at peace with my destiny.

INTERVIEWER: And what destiny is that?

CALVIN: My destiny is to enlighten the world and bring it in tune with the universe. The Sun gods decree it so. I was the chosen one; first as a Sunshine Kid, then as a performance artist. The sun is my motif and my master. It is my reason for being. First I expand my consciousness, then I illuminate – like the sun.

INTERVIEWER: Is it true that part of your act has you burning your skin while performing naked and in neon- green body paint?

CALVIN: I do not burn my flesh: I let it become one with the heat – the one true power of the sun. In that, I learn to understand and communicate telepathically with the Sun gods.

INTERVIEWER: And what do these Sun gods tell you?

CALVIN: That pain is a complicated and sacred language that
we must all learn to speak in order to enter the higher chambers
of existence. The pain that I felt as a child under those intense
lights and those more intense personal pressures was merely a
prelude to my education in the language of pain. As a child, I
selfishly resisted and resented my celestial schooling, but now I
have learned to understand both the whispers and screams of
pain and to embrace it and let it embrace me.
*
GABBI: The Mall Tour was really hard, even harder than having to record back-to-back albums in no time. It was grueling.
Singing, dancing, and then signing autograph after autograph.
We were all on autopilot. Plato kept taking speed to keep him
going, then Blake did. Then Heather. Then Benet. Then
Ronald. Then Kristy, who had such a bad reaction they had to
take her to the hospital one time. Half the cast became pint-sized
speed freaks thanks to the schedule, me included. The only one
who didn't have to sign autographs all the time was Griffen. He
got to rest up and get his dinner. The rest of us had to mingle
with all those fans. And you had to walk on eggshells. Parents
could be very cruel if they thought that you didn't give their
child enough time and attention, or if they thought your smile
wasn't bright enough in the picture.
*
NYSSA: (rolls eyes) The movie? That piece of celluloid crap?
Ugh, what a disaster! But I try to look on the Sunshine side – it
spelled the end of the show! And the beginning of my descent
into anorexia! What fun. We made that movie in like less than
ten days. On the cheap and on the fly. It should have been
named *Griffen's Undeserved and Appalling Coronation*, but those wonderful producers didn't have the balls, so they put their creative

brains together and called it *The Sunshine Kids Movie*. What a realistic flick that was. The plot was that Griffen wanted to ask a girl to the movies, but the girl was grounded because she didn't do her homework and failed a test; so then the Sunshine Kids would very naturally break into song and dance, and solve these problems by warbling on the importance of doing your homework and listening to your elders. My favorite part was that we would be completely stumped at how to solve the problem, then one of us "thought" of the answer, but then everybody would know the words and melody to the song about the previously unknown solution, and we'd dance in the same choreographed way. For those three kids gullible enough to go see that movie, I apologize that you wasted both your allowance and ninety minutes of your life that you can never get back. (laughs)
*

PITCH: Look, I'm really, really happy that I have so many wonderful fans who still fondly remember the Sunshine Kids, but I'm doing other things right now, like performing in regional theater and recording adult contemporary music. It's hard, I've composed a lot of good songs that are directed towards adults, and all the audience at the county fair is asking for, is for me to sing a medley of old Sunshine songs. I am not a children's singer and I'm not a child anymore. I haven't gone by that hurtful name "Pitch" in almost twenty years; it's Steven now. I've grown and evolved as an artist since then, really. I have a lot more mature things to say. I know a lot of thirty-something people still want me to wear the neon-yellow sweat shirt and baggy jeans and tell them to eat their vegetables, but it's like having to read the same bedtime story night after night. I've moved on, and maybe the fans should move on, too.
*

NYSSA: Griffen wouldn't give you an interview, would he?

INTERVIEWER: Well, it's too soon to say...

NYSSA: Ha! He didn't! And that psycho coward thug won't, mark my words. Mister Big Shot Has-Been has never had to answer to anyone before. He used to abuse me every day. He marked me, and then there was no escape. Cornered me in the girl's dressing room. I'm sure the producers knew, but they were grooming him for bigger things; and I was a big nobody; so nothing changed in two long, hellacious years. He used to say I deserved it because I was fat and ugly, then he'd read me all the hate mail I got to drive the point home that Nyssa was human trash; so, you know, I wouldn't have an ounce of self-esteem left. And then the director used to scream at me to smile for the cameras and called me stupid. I was scared right out of my mind. I guess his tastes for certain age groups hasn't changed in twenty years. I hope the jury nails his ass for everything's he's done. (cries)

INTERVIEWER: Are you all right?

NYSSA: Sorry, I am, I am, I'm a Sunshine Kid, remember? We're always doing supertastically great, even when we're coming on to the Grim Reaper, trying to seduce him. And we're really good at that, too, considering how many of us got the ultimate notch on our bedpost. (pauses) You just try to survive from day to day in that dark, noisy see-through box you're put in. They shove you in there, they shove you in there naked and alone, but they give you a neon-colored top and faded jeans if you want to wear 'em, but they're ten sizes too small. It's been the no-choice choice from Day One, and it hasn't changed for me. I'll be on my deathbed and the last thing I'll think about will be those stupid lyrics to that stupid song:
(sings)   *Betcha you wish you were that kid.*
          Betcha you dream to be that kid.
          Betcha you wish you were a Sunshine Kid!

The Birthday Boy of Bingford

I

The party guests were getting bored, weepy, and restless, but they were willing to endure the painful and prolonged routine until dessert arrived. It was something about licking the thick neon-green cake icing that made their patient gallantry worthwhile; besides, homework and bedtime hours weren't negotiable, either. The reluctant visitors were used to living captive, disjointed lives and their battle scars showed up readily in their attire: loose socks, open flies, runny noses, bruised knees, messy pigtails, and dirty fingernails all declared that this crowd was a tough bunch. The entire affair was as boring as last year's party, though their teachers and parents repeatedly assured them this festivity would be a "fun thing to do."

So far, the grownup's promises were so far off the mark that one had to wonder about the adults' accounts about the benefits of eating vegetables, and even the veracity of Santa Claus, too. Where was the fun? The stale air and the squirmish crush of antsy guests made the large room seem strangely small and stifling. The sun-faded red, blue, and green streamers had holes and dust and the helium balloons were as appealing as lumpy, overripe fruit. The back of the room was the tidiest corner, with a table dotted with small but expensive slices of shocking green, pink, red, blue, purple, and yellow cake all neatly aligned in perfect rows according to color, size, and price. The room's lighting was as bright as the cakes' colors and old, matte confetti lay lifeless on the scratched tiled floor.

On the podium stood a middle-aged man and a woman behind the wooden dais: the man was short and stocky with an oily black hairpiece lying awkwardly on his round, red head. He was wearing a white suit and tie and a large name tag proclaiming in big black letters that he was "Mayor C. Cole Capshaw." The woman beside him was somewhat younger and more alert. She was tall and slim; her red suit looked expensive and sinister, as if it were protecting its angular contents. Her blue eyes pierced souls like talons and her backside seemed to be made of stone. Her perky, vicious smile revealed a mouth full of white, obedient teeth and her blonde hair was coifed in a stiff, disciplined style. Both the man and the woman seemed too cheery for the occasion.

"Now, kids," said the man as he pointed his stubby, red index finger to a figure sitting beside the podium, "won't you all join me in singing a very special Happy Birthday to Bingford's most famous birthday boy?"

A small, collective, and resigned sigh oozed from the audience. All the guests felt embarrassed and reluctant, but joined in the familiar chorus.

"Happeee birthdaaay toooo yoooou! Happeee birthdaaay toooo yoooou! Happeee birthdaaay deeeear Birthday Boy! Happeee birthdaaay toooo yoooou!"

The halfhearted obligatory applause followed as more sighs and complaints bubbled to the front of the room. The guests already felt the party had dragged on even longer than last year's: the museum tour took twenty minutes longer than twelve months ago and the parade had three new floats and a battalion of perky baton twirlers with plastic, red and pink strawberry charms framing their ponytails. But at least there was only one more song to sing and one more story to listen to before cake and ice cream would be served.

The ruddy man with the white suit and big name tag still seemed happy as he continued speaking to his captive audience: "What wonderful singers you kids are! Now let's ask how old the Birthday Boy is this year, boys and girls."

The Birthday Boy in question was drooping and squirming in his birthday chair beside the podium: it was an old, red- and-gold throne, though the red cushions were frayed, flat, and faded, and the gold paint was dulled and peeling from the wooden frame. The man's old, wrinkly face sagged in boredom and resignation; it was as if he had long ago lost any enthusiasm and lust for his own special day. The Birthday Boy's long, frail, and lanky frame looked as bored and resigned as did his sullen, lined face. The ashen man appeared even more ghostly with his gold paper crown resting crookedly on his small, bald head. His lime-green polyester trousers lay uneasily on his twitching body, as did his matching dinner jacket and bow tie. The face, the back, the arms, the legs, and even the feet seemed disjointed from each other, but all his parts looked as desperate to leave the room as did the young guests.

At the repeated urging of the man and the woman on the stage, the impatient chorus began to sing a little faster and curter than before: "How old are you now? How old are you now? How ooo-old are you now-oww? How old are you now?"

The tepid and melodic query was met by a tired, but dutiful voice that warbled into the microphone softly as it wheezed: "I'm a hundred an' two! I'm a hundred an' two! I'm a hundred an' twooo-ooo an' a lot older than you!"

"Waaaaahh!! No, you're not!" a disgruntled little wail protested amid indignant and whiny tears.

The song was topped with more soft, bored applause mixed in with throat-clearing, shuffling, and general churlish whining. No one, it appeared, was having fun.

"Now, Birthday Boy," the man with the wig and white suit said in a perky and patronizing tone, "make a wish and blow out the candle!"

On cue, a stout young black man wearing a lime-green polyester bow tie with matching slacks and dinner jacket came out from the back door and begrudgingly headed to the red and gold throne. The chubby young man, who looked no older than twenty, dragged himself over to the Birthday Boy with a small lime-green frosted birthday cake with a single lit candle protruding on top. The cake holder looked bored, embarrassed, and restless as he rolled his eyes and somewhat abruptly and impudently shoved the birthday cake in front of the guest of honor.

"Here, Birthday Boy," the young man muttered with a tinge of faux enthusiasm, "blow out the candle and make a wish or something."

"Okay," said the Birthday Boy deferentially.

Filling his lungs with the stale room air, the old man's wrinkly face expanded and stretched until he inhaled enough wind for the task ahead. Then slowly, he began to blow out his candle. At first, the stubborn flame bent, but did not dissipate. The old man frowned and refilled his aged lungs once again, this time with more ardor. Looking determined, the old man with the bow tie blew at the candle with all his might. The flame bent horizontally, waving its light like a flag in the wind for a brief moment, before it flung itself vertically on top of the candle.

The old man looked at his audience: the guests looked agitated, as did the cake holder and the man and woman on stage. With a weak smile, he filled his sore lungs with air and blew at the candle once more. With a jolt of passion, the Birthday Boy hurled a gust of wind toward the candle; then, suddenly, his dentures flew from his crinkly and thin mouth and landed on top of the birthday cake. With the sudden motion of the disembodied teeth and gums, the yellow flicker crowning the candle disappeared.

"Ewwww!" a disgusted chorus of small, shrill voices yelled in unison.

"I'm not eating *that* cake!"

"That's gross!"

"Yuck!"

"Waaaaahh!"

"Mommy! His teeth fell out!"

"I don't want my teeth to fall out, too!"

"Children! Please settle down," the man with the white suit said somewhat curtly as he glared at the young black man. The young man scrunched his nose, then with some facial expression of disgust, removed the offending dentures from the cake with his thumb and index finger, and returned them to their rightful owner. The old man looked around the room before he reclaimed his teeth with his shaky, thin hand and placed them back into his mouth.

"Now, Birthday Boy," the woman with the forced smile and rock hard buttocks began to enunciate deliberately, "tell the children how you became world-famous for your birthday!"

The old man with the paper crown and loose teeth sat up in his chair with some effort. "Well, Denise," the Birthday Boy began, "over a hundred years ago, my parents lived in Bingford and owned just about every business in town. They had plenty of money and a lot of nice things, but they weren't happy because they were missin' somethin'. My parents always wanted to have children, you see. For years and years and years they wanted kids. Used to make my mother cry all the time because she was forty-four and didn't have no children. Then one day, she got in a family way and nine months later, I was born and my parents were so happy, they wanted to share their joy with everybody in the world." The old man's wet cough interrupted his narrative before he regained his composure and continued.

"And when I turned one, my mother and father threw me the biggest birthday party you ever saw and invited everyone who wanted to come to join in the celebration and everyone could have some cake and ice cream. Then they did it every year after that and the parties just got bigger and bigger, until one day one of them big city papers wrote about my birthday parties – then them big parties got really big and the city got involved, too. Even after my folks passed on, Bingford still celebrated my birthday and everybody 'round the world liked it so much, the town decided to do it more often. So, now four times a year, I get a nice birthday party and all the little boys and girls come for cake an' ice cream. And that's how I became the Birthday Boy of Bingford!"

"Thank you for that lovely story, Birthday Boy," the woman on the stage chirped as she focused her intense blue eyes on the old man on the throne and began to clap.

As some of the guests followed the intense woman's lead in a tepid round of applause, others had lost their patience altogether:

"Mommy, the Birthday Boy is scary!"

"I wanna go home!"

"Waaaaahh.!"

"I hafta go to the bathwoom!"

"I'm not a booger brain!"

"Are too!"

"This is boring."

"Why do we have to come here every year? I'm in medical school now."

"I hate the Birthday Boy."

"Ewwww! Billy peed his pants!"

"If you don't stop whining, we're going home."

"His teeth fell out!"

"What do you mean you don't want to take your picture with the Birthday Boy? Why did I drive five hours here for?"

"And remember, kids," the woman on stage said brightly with a venomous smile, "after you take your very own picture with Bingford's very special Birthday Boy, the gift shop has a two for one special on Birthday Boy lollipops, and Birthday Boy watches are twenty percent off!"

It took almost another two hours before all the guests hopped on the Birthday Boy's knee for their photograph and bought their slice of cake and scoop of ice cream. The persistent complaints and whining were met with increasingly severe parental admonishments and threats, while the man and woman on stage continued to nod their heads and display their frozen grins. It was early evening when all of the guests finally left the party. The only ones remaining were the Birthday Boy, the young cake holder, the man with the white suit, and the woman with the firm buttocks and baleful smile.

The old man with the ersatz crown slowly rose from his chair. He look around the room, frowned, and pulled the paper crown off his head as he examined his pant legs. Looking at a wide, wet stain on his left leg, the old man shook his crooked little finger at the remaining occupants of the room.

"Stupid little brat," he wheezed as he got up and pointed to his pant leg with his other hand.

No one acknowledged his outrage. The young man was too busy drinking his soda and fixing his short dreadlocks. The man in the white suit was somberly reading over some documents. The woman was rummaging through her briefcase, looking for her cigarillos.

"Stupid little brat," the old man in the green polyester suit snarled again. "Pissed on my good slacks. That's disgusting and it's ain't no way for some poor old man to be living his final years."

"Ritchie, stop whining, will you?" said the man in the white suit. "At least none of those kids puked on your shoes this time. That has to be a first."

"Capshaw's right," noted the woman as she found her cigarillos, "I don't know what's the big deal, anyway. You get paid to sit on your skinny little ass and sing Happy Birthday. You get a house, fame, four fabulous parties a year, and a sitter. You're swimming in gravy, you disgusting little ingrate. Most people would kill for that. So some rug rat spills his lunch on you – get over yourself."

"I hate when they piss on my leg. It makes me sick to my stomach," whined the Birthday Boy.

"Cry me a river, you mangy old man; I've got my own problems – you try working for Jared Smythe. And another thing," Denise hissed as she lit a cigarillo, "what's with your damned dentures falling out like that? You moron caused a scene for nothing! Scaring all those little jerks right out of their soiled diapers. Those are kids! That's bad for our image and bad for business. Thank God this wasn't the big show – if the media got a hold of that scene – this whole town would be wiped off the map!"

"It ain't my fault," the old man said angrily as he shook his long crooked finger at Denise. "Homer buys my denture cream. I'm not allowed to go to the store by myself. He bought some new cream yesterday. Smells funny, too."

The woman turned to the young black man in the green suit and started to scream, "Homer Juneau, you incompetent slacker...!"

"Hey," Homer protested as he removed his clip-on bow tie, "you cut my shopping budget. I can't buy the good stuff with the bread you guys give me."

"Give me a break! How much does decent denture cream cost?"

"Hey, man," Homer snapped as he took off his jacket, "I can't buy the good denture cream, and all those skin rags and chocolate popsicles with the money you cheapskates give me."

"You're not supposed to be buying yourself dirty magazines with that money!" Denise shrieked as she jabbed her index finger into Homer's well-padded chest.

"Not for me, for Mr. Ridgley!" Homer said, pointing to the Birthday Boy.

"That's right," concurred the Birthday Boy, "I like my magazines with all those nice-looking girls. There ain't nothin' else to do around here and you won't let me go to the Torpedo Mama. I'm bored."

"But how many damned magazines is this jerk buying for you? And chocolate popsicles..."

"It's my very favorite kind," the Birthday Boy noted proudly.

"Who cares? From now on, no more popsicles and no more magazines! All that junk food can't be good for you and we don't need some kid coming across your stash of porno mags and causing a scandal. New directive, Homer: you collect and destroy every magazine in that geezer's collection..."

"Look here, Denise!" yelled the trembling Birthday Boy, "I'm a hundred an' two! I ain't got nothin' else to live for. I just sit here on an uncomfortable chair havin' to listen to all those screamin' and cryin' little brats who pee and poop and throw up on me!

An old man is entitled to somethin' nice before he dies. And I *like* my popsicles and my magazines."

"You live in this nice, big house just by wearing that stupid paper hat. You never had to work a day in your worthless life and you have the nerve to complain!"

"Let's cool it, okay," warned Capshaw somewhat nervously. "I don't want him getting a heart attack or something even worse, okay? Let's just calm down. Ritchie, the popsicles are okay – in moderation, of course, but Denise is right: those magazines can make trouble for your image and for this town. Gotta keep it clean for the kids. Find yourself another pastime, okay?"

"No, it ain't okay. I can't take it no more. I'm a hundred an' two! Why can't we have only one birthday party a year for me, like everybody else?"

"Once a year? Come on, now, Ritchie," said Capshaw in his patronizing drawl, "you know Bingford's entire economy depends on your birthday parties. We can't run this town without 'em. Now, why don't you go upstairs with Homer and he'll fix you a nice warm glass of milk before you go to bed."

"I just about had it with birthdays," the old man protested with a wrinkly fist in the air as he left the room with Homer. "They make me sick."

Capshaw shook his head as he gathered his papers. "He's getting worse every year. It's getting harder to control him."

"Controlling him and his image is my job. You leave that bitching old bag of bones to me. I'll set him straight, all right."

"You watch it, Denise. I don't want that old man dropping dead on the account of you terrorizing him. It's bad enough you have a big turnover with your staff."

"Those good for nothing morons couldn't hack it. We don't need wusses who burn out in three months, dammit. You think running a PR company is easy? Dammit, just look at this account: trying to make some dirty old man seem cute and cuddly."

"But, I have to admit you and your team do an excellent job of it."

Denise grabbed her briefcase and started to head out the door. "Of course I do. That's what Jared Smythe pays me for, Capshaw. Now, if you'll excuse me, I have to make sure the new ad campaign is ready to go. Christ!"

II

It was the day before the "big one": the Birthday Boy's "real" birthday party. Ridgley's one hundred and third birthday was sure to be largest party yet. Many reporters and photographers had already descended to Bingford as did tourists who had flown in with their young children to join in the festivities. Their various needs, from diapers to technical support were met with typical Bingfordian politeness and efficiency.

Sitting behind her desk at the "Birthday Mansion" was Denise, going over the schedule for tomorrow's party along with Mayor Capshaw who was seated in a plush chair across from her.

"Everything seems to be in order for tomorrow. Even the weather's supposed to be nice. Not too humid. A perfect August day for a birthday party. That always helps attendance," noted Capshaw.

"What helps attendance is my impeccable planning and genius – and don't you ever forget that," snapped Denise as she glared at Capshaw.

"I didn't mean to imply that you weren't an excellent promoter and marketer..."

"Well, I am and I'd appreciate it if you'd acknowledge my prowess before you acknowledge the weather..."

A gravelly baritone voice and the whiff of strong cigar smoke crashed in on the conversation. "Denise Smother-Tucker, you were always such a shameless braggart."

"Who the hell said that?" Denise yelled as she turned around to face her detractor. "Oh, it's just you, Jared."

Jared Smythe stood in the doorway for a brief second before he sauntered inside and regally acknowledged his associates with a slight, but confident nod. Jared was a tall, well-built man who indulged in his dark, rugged good looks. His long salt-and-pepper hair was as well-tended as his granite pressed suit and white, buttoned shirt. Even the wrinkles and lines on his face worked hard to make their owner look attractive.

"Everything seems to be going smoothly this time. The food and souvenirs are in order, I hear. What about the Birthday Boy? Is he ready for tomorrow?" Jared asked as he sat down in a chair next to Capshaw.

Denise scrunched her nose as she frowned. "Of course he's ready. What other responsibilities does that moron have? We just had a dress rehearsal this morning and he knows his lines. Dammit, if we could just keep that repulsive relic in check. He's getting to be a real pain in the ass. Still carrying on about some kid taking a leak on his leg and then griping about losing all his magazines. It doesn't seem to matter what anyone says or does, he just pounds his decrepit little fist on the table and screeches like a baboon. He quiets down only if I let him have it, but even then he gets all upset. I've got better things to do than discipline some old jerk."

"We don't want him too upset," cautioned Jared as he took another long drag from his cigar, "after all, the big show's tomorrow and all the media will be there. The Big one-o-three. The real birthday, as that old coot calls it. I want it to be bigger and better than last year's. Have you finalized everything, Denise?"

"Of course I have. We got some B-list country singer from a town near Bingford to sing at the opening ceremony. We've added two more floats for the parade, plus there's going to be a dinner show with some old retired soap opera star starring as

Ritchie: a musical about the origins of the Birthday Boy. That shouldn't be too long. Other than that, everything is pretty much the same."

"How are the acts? Have you seen them?"

"They stink. But who gives a damn? It's just kids, what do they know? The parents bring them here for a dose of wholesomeness. Besides, it's cheaper than the amusement park."

"That's a benefit," nodded Jared while he leafed through a pile of brochures on Denise's desk and began to reminisce. "Attendance has improved substantially ever since I hired your firm to promote Birthday Boy events. You know, the Birthday Boy was always a big deal around these parts, ever since I can remember. Of course, it wasn't as big as it is now, but it wasn't really organized. Darrin and Louella, Ritchie's folks, used to invite anyone for free cake and ice cream; so that's why all the little kids came over. Then, when Ritchie grew up, City Hall took over the parties for the publicity, but City Hall being what it is lost money on it. It didn't matter all that much since the Ridgleys were wealthy and kept this town afloat. But then they sold every business they had and when they passed on, everybody was in trouble. The mayor back then got desperate and started to push the only asset Bingford had − its birthday boy..."

"And they couldn't make it work until you blew back into town and bought the rights to the Birthday Boy?"

"I'm boring you again, aren't I? But to answer your question, yes, soon after, I made it a bona fide tourist attraction, and could start rebuilding this place with the money. But you, my dear, have made it into the childhood milestone and media pilgrimage it is today, though that's not to say there isn't room for improvement..."

A frenzied rhythmic knock interrupted Jared's musings, followed by a slam. Denise, Capshaw, and Jared looked at the door. It was a frenzied, wild-eyed Homer.

"We got serious trouble!" screamed Homer as he ran inside the office.

"What's the problem now, dammit? Ritchie lose his teeth again?" Denise barked.

"No. It's worse. The Birthday Boy is dead!"

III

A frantic Homer lead Denise, Capshaw, and Jared to the body in the living room. Denise pushed her way ahead of Homer, while Capshaw twitched and walked behind the frightened young man. Jared, trailing his associates, opted to wait outside the living room door.

Denise shook her head as she examined the green-polyester-suited body lying spread eagle on the living room floor. "So what exactly happened, Homer? You're supposed to keep an eye on him; so how is it that Ritchie's dead, you big stupid idiot!"

"Hey look, man, it's not my fault he's dead! You made him upset. He probably had a heart attack because of you. He's been trippin' ever since you took his skin rags away from him. He's been impossible to live with. Always ranting that his rights are being violated and pounding his fist on the table. I couldn't take it anymore; so I left him to throw his little tantrum all by himself after dress rehearsal this morning and when I came back a few minutes ago, this is how I found him."

"For hours? You mean to say you left him alone for hours?"

"Hey, I can't just sit around and hold his skinny hand all day long, I got my singing career to think about. I don't wanna be the Birthday Boy's baby-sitter for the rest of my life, man!"

"He's a hundred and three years old, stupid!"

"Still, man, I gotta think ahead. I went out to cut a demo. It was a wasted trip. I got into a fight with the guy who was supposed to lend me his drum machine, and then he got mad at me and left. I was so mad, I went to the Macho Nacho to drown my sorrows in processed cheese. When I came back, I found him just like that."

Capshaw examined the body with a shudder. "Yeah, he looks dead to me. Angry as hell, but dead. So, now what?"

"Get Jared Smythe in here," Denise spat as she lit a cigarillo and kicked the motionless Birthday Boy, "this is his little cash cow!"

Reluctantly, Jared walked into the room and winced as he saw the pale, lifeless man on the floor. "I always hated looking at dead things. Ugh, that's him all right, that shriveled-up old prune. But he must have been mad about something before he died. Look at his face."

"Who cares about his face! What happens next?" snapped Denise as she began to pace.

There was a moment of silence before Capshaw sighed. "So what are we going to do with Ritchie? I guess one of us should make an announcement and funeral arrangements..."

"Are you out of your mind, man?" Jared snapped as he shook his cigar at Capshaw. "All my investments – this entire town's survival is pinned on the Birthday Boy. No one can know about this!"

"But the big party's tomorrow! We can't hide this kind of thing from the public. They come here to see the Birthday Boy; if he doesn't show up, they'll know something's wrong. We have to let them know..."

"Don't you realize this whole damn town's survival is dependent on the Birthday Boy juggernaut? This little backwards hellhole has no resources – nothing! No agriculture, no factories, no beauty, no industry, no charm, no convenience. No Birthday Boy, no Bingford! If wasn't for that old relic's birthday, Bingford would have gone belly-up decades ago. We're not like Turkeytown! If a turkey dies, by gum, they can always find themselves another turkey! Those vultures can't wait until we lose our crown jewel. We don't have another Birthday Boy in the popper. He was it!"

"So, Jared, what do we do?"

"We need to find another Birthday Boy and pronto – we have the big show tomorrow."

"Ritchie was an institution! People are not going to warm up to another Birthday Boy. They'll see any heir apparent as a little usurper."

"No! We have to make the public think it's Ritchie."

"What? Are you suggesting we dress up some poor old schmoe and pass him off as Ridgley?"

"Exactly."

"How are we going to find a look-alike on such short notice? The party's tomorrow. He has to be groomed and trained. There's no way we can do that on that kind of tight time frame!"

"It's a gamble, but at this point we have no choice but to try. There's a nursing home up the block. There has to be some wrinkled old prune that fits the bill."

"But what do we do with Ritchie?"

"We need to hide his body – we can't let anyone see it or it's good-bye Bingford."

"Do you know what you're suggesting?! That's outrageous,"

screamed Capshaw.

"Do you want the media or some little kid to find his corpse and cause a scandal? They won't believe an impostor is the real deal when the real deal is lying here dead on the floor!"

"So where do we hide Ritchie?" asked Denise as she stared at the corpse by her feet.

"I know where we can stash it until tomorrow, " sighed Jared. "There's the florist shop – De Flowers. That's Hanna Barbara Herman-Helfer's shop. She doesn't care too much for me or for people investing in the Birthday Boy, but at least her shop has a big freezer room where she keeps her wares. We could wrap up Ritchie and put him in her freezer until after the party tomorrow. But she would never play a part in this; we'll have to sneak the body in there and not tell her."

"And hope to God she doesn't stumble upon it," blurted Capshaw.

"I know it's a big gamble, but she's not the most observant person in town. Let Homer take Ritchie there, while the rest of us work on finding a replacement."

Homer looked up. "Me? Why should I risk a rap sheet?"

"Because if you don't, you'll be safer in jail than being on the outside with me," spat Denise. "Just be careful and don't get caught."

"Use the back door, Homer," warned Jared as he fixed his jacket collar. "Then go out to the back of Hanna Barbara's store when it gets a little darker. The freezer room is on the left. Hide it in the back corner – she doesn't use the entire room. Make sure no one sees you."

Homer grumbled beneath his breath as he began to drag Ritchie by the feet. "I'm sick and tired of doing all the dirty work. I want a raise for this." With some effort, he dragged the body out of the room, while muttering various disturbing and revolting obscenities. The sounds of bumping and cursing slowly tapered to a dead silence.

Jared straightened out his jacket with a firm tug at the edges. "I have a meeting with a few dignitaries this evening. I can't cancel since they came with their children for tomorrow's party. I can't rouse any suspicions. I'll leave the replacement hunting to the two of you. I'll see you later."

Before either Denise or Capshaw could protest, Jared quickly left. Denise grabbed her briefcase and left for her car with Capshaw following hurriedly and apprehensively behind her. Moments later, Denise and Capshaw left the mansion and headed for the short drive to the somewhat dilapidated Atropos Nursing Home. Denise quickly shut off her engine and jumped out of her car, while Capshaw paused to look at the peeling paint and broken pavement. He could barely catch up as Denise had already walked inside the home.

The inside of the building was even more run-down than the facade: old sun-faded furniture clutched and cradled gnarled bodies with closed eyes and telescoped backs. The wallpaper and carpets housed various stains and torn edges. Capshaw slouched as he shook his head.

"What are we doing here?" he asked as he disapprovingly inhaled the smells of body odors, ointments, and food.

"What do you think, you big stupid idiot? We're here to look for our replacement Birthday Boy, that's what," Denise snapped in an undertone. "No wonder this stupid little town is so screwed up – it's got itself a stupid little mayor. Let's take a look at the pickings here. If anyone can pass for Ritchie, we nab him. Leave the talking to me."

The pickings were slim, indeed, thought Capshaw as he scoured the room for a promising replacement. But the odds were against them: first, the vast majority of candidates were female and this was no time for equal opportunity. Some of the candidates were in wheelchairs or using walkers: another drawback. Those who were rambling about the government or calling for their mothers had to be rejected, too. This left him with only a handful of promising recruits.

"What about this one?" he asked, pointing to a man playing solitaire at a table.

"Too fat and bloated. Besides, he's missing his two front teeth."

"That one looks kind of like Ritchie..."

"He's Asian," screamed Denise. "Let me look, all right? You can't do anything right."

Denise's devious eyes began to stalk and hunt. Capshaw looked at his companion closely until a flash of discovery beamed from her face. "He'll do," she said to herself. "Let's go talk to him."

The old man in question was sitting in a rocking chair, reading the town's newspaper. Capshaw studied him closely. The man was probably Ritchie's height and build, though there were differences. This man seemed to be twenty years younger than Ritchie, darker, and somewhat fatter. His thick white hair also seemed problematic. But the eye color matched, and at this point, beggars couldn't be choosers.

Denise sat beside the old man and smiled.

"Hello," she chirped kindly. "What are you reading?"

"The Bingford Beaver," said the man proudly as he looked up at Denise, "I've been reading the Beaver for sixty years. Never miss a day. Have to know what's going on in town."

"You seem very smart," noted Denise sweetly. "What's your name?"

"My name is Clement Gotch."

"Really? I'm Denise, and this is Mayor Capshaw."

The old man squinted as he took a closer look at Denise's companion. "Why, it is! Hello, Mayor Capshaw. How are you today?"

"I'm fine," muttered Capshaw nervously. "We'd like to talk to you for a few minutes."

"What about?" asked the old man nervously. "Am I in trouble?"

"Not at all," laughed Denise as she patted him on the shoulder, "In fact, we have some very good news for you. Do you mind to answer a couple of questions for the mayor?"

"I guess not," shrugged Clement, still uncertain about his sudden visitors.

"How old are you? Are you in good health?"

"I'm eighty-seven and in pretty good health. Why does the mayor need to know that?"

"We're giving a prize and we have to know for our records," said Denise. "Do you have any family around here?"

"Not here. They live in Turkeytown. I got a daughter and a grandson named Nermal – he's eighteen years old. His mama never said who his father was, but Nermal's a real nice and good-looking boy and he means the world to me, but his mama says he ain't right in the head. Mind you, he ain't the smartest boy in town, but then again, his mama is a real mean woman..."

"Yeah, yeah," snapped a peeved and impatient Denise. "Look, do you want to stay in this old people's orphanage for the rest of your life or do you want to live in a nice big mansion with a staff and wonderful parties?"

"I'd like to live in a nice house, but I'm old. I can't take of the chores; my knees don't work like they used to."

"You'd have people who'd take care of that for you. All you have to do is follow our orders, starting tomorrow go to four parties a year in your home, and not tell anybody about this agreement. What do you say?"

"Why shouldn't I say anything?"

"Because if you do, everybody else will want a piece of this generous offer and then there will be nothing left for you or your family. Well, are you interested?"

Clement pondered then nodded. "Sounds fine to me..."

"Terrific, now sign here," Denise said nonchalantly as she pulled a pen and contract from her briefcase and handed them to the old man.

Clement looked uneasily at Denise. "What's this?"

"It's our standard non-disclosure agreement," dismissed Denise.

"I don't like the sound of any phrase that I don't know what it means," replied Clement suspiciously. "Signing things with fancy words always means trouble. Contracts are for fat cats who want to boss around the mice."

"Clement, think of your grandson Nermal," Denise cooed sympathetically, "If he's developmentally delayed or whatever the hell's wrong with him, don't you think it's your duty to provide for him long after your gone?"

"Nermal ain't slow," protested Clement somewhat angrily. "But it's just that his mama says he ain't right in the head, but she won't tell me how. I can't tell what's wrong, though; he looks okay t'me. He's very polite and kind. Nice t'animals, too."

"What difference does it make?" Denise hissed while trying to control her rage. "Don't you want to provide for your family and live your reclining years in comfort? This contract will ensure that you provide for him in the right way. It prevents anyone from breaking promises and destroying your grandson's future."

Clement considered. "Well, I guess you got a point there, miss."

"Of course, I have a point! Now sign this contract."

As the old man took the pen to paper with his frail, trembling hand, he carefully signed on the lines marked "X." He returned the pen to Denise and looked at her curiously. "There. Now, what do I have to do?"

"First, you come with us to your new house. When we get there, you'll go through orientation. But hurry up, we haven't got all day."

"I have to get back to City Hall," said Capshaw as he walked out of the room.

"What for? To meet with one of your bimbos?"

"Something like that. I'll see you in the Birthday Mansion first thing tomorrow. Bye for now."

When Denise and Clement arrived at the Birthday Mansion, both Homer and Jared were already waiting: Jared was tense, but alert, while Homer was nervous as he sat on the sofa, biting his lip and fixing his hair. Jared looked at Clement and nodded approvingly.

"Good choice," he said, nodding as he smoked his cigar. "Dinner finished early; so I decided to come back here and see how things were progressing."

"They're progressing as good as can be expected under the circumstances. Well, Homer," Denise asked tersely as she lead Clement to a chair in the living room, "did you move him to Hanna Barbara's as you were told?"

"Yeah," Homer moped, "I did. It was a clunky job, but lucky for me Ms. Herman-Helfer wasn't around. Everything was unlocked; so I just dragged him in, covered him up with a sheet, and put him in the farthest corner. You can't see him unless you go behind some boxes and it doesn't look like anyone's been there for ages. He should hold until tomorrow. But what if she finds him before then?"

"She won't," Jared interjected. "She keeps saying that refrigerator room is too big and that she only uses about half of it. She's too busy thinking about her various causes to notice it, anyway."

"So that's settled," Denise said as she took a cigarillo out of her briefcase and lit it.

"Not everything's settled, ma'am," interjected Clement sternly, but politely, "you still haven't told me what it is I have to do to live here in the Birthday Mansion."

"What do you think, stupid? You have to pretend that you're Ritchie Ridgley, the Birthday Boy of Bingford."

"What? The Birthday Boy? Why do you want me to make up a story like that?"

"Because the Birthday Boy can't do it anymore."

"Why is that? Is he ill?"

Denise put out her cigarillo in annoyance. "He doesn't want to make little boys and girls like your Nermal happy anymore. See, that's bad for Bingford. And you want Bingford to be a good place for your grandson to live, right?

"But he lives in Turkeytown, ma'am."

"Who cares? You are to do what we tell you, understood? From now on, you tell people that you are Ritchie Ridgley, the Birthday Boy of Bingford, who is celebrated worldwide because he is the most special birthday boy of all. Now, Clement," Denise asked sternly as she stared furiously at the timid old man with her cold eyes, "what's your name?"

"Clement," the old man answered dutifully," Clement Gotch."

"No, you idiot! Your goddamn name is Ritchie! Ritchie Ridgley! Got that?"

"No, it ain't," the old man protested angrily before he felt his body rise. He looked up; Denise's fierce scowl cornered his face and her wiry hands clenched his plaid shirt and lifted him several inches from his chair.

"If you want to live to see another birthday, you better start coughing up the answers I want to hear! Now, what was your name again?"

"Ritchie Ridgley," Clement whispered timidly.

"And what makes you special?" barked Denise as she lifted Clement even higher from his chair.

"I got a birthday," the old man wheezed as his lower lip quivered.

"That's a start," Denise growled as she let go of Clement. With a dull thud, the old man fell back into his chair and whimpered.

"Homer," Denise yelled as she firmly grabbed the young man by the arm, "get some tweezers and start plucking that old coot's hair."

"What the –? You want me to pluck his hair? All of it?"

"That's what I said."

"What the hell for?"

"Because Ritchie was bald, you dumb stupid moron. See, that's bad. The Birthday Boy is bald. This old geezer's got a head full of white hair." Denise grabbed a handful of Clement's snowy mane with her free hand and gave it a tug toward Homer as if to emphasize her point.

"Owww!" screamed Clement.

Denise ignored the old man. "He'll never pass muster. He has to look bald, dammit!"

"Then just shave it off or something."

"Stubble, stupid, stubble! If we shave it; he might grow some stubble by tomorrow. We can't afford stubble. It's too telltale."

"Then shave it tomorrow! I'm not plucking any old guy's hair with tweezers!"

Denise tightened her grip on Homer's arm as she flashed an angry sneer. "No good. We don't have time to shave his head tomorrow. It has to be tweezed. Right now."

"The whole thing is whacked," Homer pouted as he shuffled his feet.

"Who asked you? Now get those damn tweezers and start plucking his damn head. I haven't got all day!" She pushed Homer toward the door.

"It's stupid..."
"Now!"

"Man, you're a heartless bitch."

"What did you say to me?"

"Nothing."

"Then go get the tweezers."

"Okay, okay..." Homer sighed as he left the room to look for tweezers.

"And something else," Denise said slowly as she turned to look at a pacing Jared, "We need a girdle – that old coot has to be at least twenty pounds heavier than Ritchie. We have to make him look thinner."

Jared considered as he scratched his salt-and-pepper hair. "What about Angelique LaFleur?"

"What about that slut?" Denise growled as she frowned.

"Well, she's a stripper at the Torpedo Mama. Pretty little thing, too. She's gotta have herself all sorts of frilly contraptions like that."

"And she's one fly girl, that's for sure," Homer chimed as he returned to the room with a pair of tweezers and headed straight for Clement. "Okay, grampaw, this is gonna hurt some. I still don't know why we can't just shave it off."

He began to pluck Clement's hairline clumsily, tugging each hair three or four times before he pulled every hair from the old man's head.
"Owww!" Clement repeatedly screamed.

"This is stupid," Homer griped between plucks, "why can't we just tell everyone that Mr. Ridgley kicked the bucket? Here I am, an aspiring superstar, forced to pluck some old dude like he's some turkey just to make ends meet!"

"Shut up and keep tweezing! Do you want our entire economy to go down the toilet?" Denise screamed. As she regained her composure, she carefully studied Clement, shaking her head disapprovingly. "Clement's too dark. We need to get some make-up to lighten up his complexion."

"I'm not putting any make-up on no old man!" Homer yelled.

"Owww, it hurts!" screamed Clement as he began to cry.

"Of course you are, and make sure you do a good job of it, unless you want to be out of job. It's your damn fault Ridgley's gone, you sloppy good-for-nothing. Jared, get someone to fetch Angelique's girdle. See if she has any stage make-up, too. We still have a lot of work to do."

IV

The day of the "real" birthday party was always full of worries, thought Capshaw as he waited nervously in the media relations room in the Birthday Mansion. Ritchie would complain about the children and the restrictions; Jared would complain about the bottom line; and Denise would terrify her staff and anyone else in the vicinity. But now Ritchie was dead and his body stashed in a florist's freezer and his replacement was essentially a senile hostage. Could Denise and Jared really pull this off? The odds were against them: for one, this time the media would be there, snapping pictures. For another, there wasn't enough time to properly groom and train the new Birthday Boy. Untested commodities, as a general rule, could never live up to a well-rehearsed veteran. But for Capshaw, the most frightening prospect was if Ms. Herman-Helfer stumbled upon Ritchie's frozen corpse.

But the wheels were already in motion. Capshaw anxiously adjusted his hairpiece as he looked at Denise. "Do you think that old geezer's ready? Do you think he'll pass muster and all that?"

"He better be ready," spat Denise as she lit up her cigarillo. "Or he's going to find his other foot in the grave."

"Denise!"

"I don't mean literally, you stupid moron! What do you take me for? Anyway, where's Jared and Clement?"

Jared walked inside as he heard his name. "I'm here. Have you seen the replacement yet? How does he look?"

"We haven't seen the final product yet," Denise groused as she paced the room. "But, just to be safe, we'll keep the lighting darker than usual and we won't let the media come close to him.

That ought to help our case, in any rate. Christ, I hope that idiot didn't screw things up."

It was less than ten minutes when a loud, rhythmic knock danced on the door. "We're here!" chimed Homer. In the background, an old voice could be heard simpering.

"Get him in here now, Homer," Denise yelled as she opened the door. Her eyes widened as she looked at Homer and the elderly man weeping beside him.

Her face reddened as she screamed, "He looks like a goddamn freak! Look at that make-up – it's totally sloppy. What's with this kabuki look, anyway?"

"Don't blame me," Homer protested, "I'm no Max Factor. That's the only stuff I got – I can't make magic with grease paint."

"Can it," Denise screeched.

"Why are his eyes so red and swollen?" asked Capshaw.

"He was crying the whole time I was plucking his head."

Capshaw stood over the old man, frowning. "Speaking of which, just look at his head! It's all raw and bumpy."

"Bleedy, too," nodded Jared.

"Well? What did you expect? Can't pluck all that hair just like that! I told you we should have shaved it off."

"But why did you pluck his head? Why didn't you just use hair removal cream? That's what my wife uses for her legs," Capshaw said as he took a closer look at Clement's sore, red scalp.

"I hate the whole world," wept Clement.

"And look at his figure," yelled Denise, "he's got curves now and big boobs – like a woman! What did you do to him?"

"Hey, man, don't go dumping on me; he's wearing one of Angelique's girdles – it's got some kind of padded bra or something."

"Then get some scissors and cut off the padding!"

"Can't do that. That's the most expensive girdle Angelique owns and she says she wants it back the same way she gave it to us. She said she'd tell the media what you guys were up to if you wrecked her favorite piece of lingerie."

"Who told her about what happened to Ritchie?" screamed Denise.

"I did," Homer said sheepishly and winced. "I thought she already knew..."

"You stupid moron! You should know better than to blabber to that bimbo! A woman who is loose with her body is loose with her lips, too. The whole world is going to know before the end of the day. I can't believe you told her the Birthday Boy is dead!"

"The Birthday Boy is dead?" gasped a shocked Clement. "You people tricked me!"

"What do you want from me?" asked Homer, ignoring the faux Birthday Boy. "I can't keep all this straight; I have an audition tomorrow at some club and I gotta get in the right groove."

60

"You people tricked me! You said nothing about no torture or killing the real Birthday Boy. I have been cruelly used! I am going to tell the proper authorities what you people done to me," cried Clement.

"Shut up, old fool. You signed that non-disclosure agreement. Do you know what that means?"

"No," quivered Clement.

"It means if you tell anyone what happened, you will spend the rest of your life in jail. Now do you understand?"

"Yes," cried Clement.

"Homer, you are going to pay for this! If you can't cut the pads, then at least tape them down," Denise vented and gritted her snow-white teeth before she turned her attentions to Clement. "Forget it. Now, Birthday Boy, we're going to go over this one more time: what do you say when the kids ask how old are you now?"

"I'm a hundred and two..."

"No, you moron! You sing, "I'm hundred an' three and you're all a lot younger than me. Got it?"

"I can't remember all that. My head is sore," Clement blubbered.

"You better remember. The show's about to start. Homer, go take the Birthday Boy to the throne. Capshaw and I are going on stage."

"Come on, grampaw, it's show time," Homer sighed as he took

Clement by the arm and lead him to the birthday room.

"I have been tricked and abused! You people are worse than my daughter."

"Yeah, yeah, just keep quiet and play along; you already got me into enough trouble as it is."

Homer opened the large blue door and lead the puling old man to the throne. As Clement sat on the faded red-and- gold chair, Homer grabbed the paper crown from a nearby table and placed it on the old man's head. Homer shook his head as he looked around the room.

"Hey, man, it sure is dark in here. The photographers are going to complain for sure. We'll never pull this off."

"You people should be reported to the proper authorities," screamed Clement.

"Shhh! Do you want to screw the whole thing up? Just play along and they'll leave you alone for the next three months."

"You mean I have to be plucked again?"

"Shhh! Don't yell or Denise will kill both of us."

"Is that why she killed the Birthday Boy?"

"Shhh!"

Within minutes, the weary young guests were escorted to the birthday room. Moments later, the sides of the room were lined by a scrum of antsy reporters and photographers waiting to take pictures and videos of the Birthday Boy. Most of the reporters were either embarrassed young journalists earning their stripes or bitter ones who were sent here as punishment for various journalistic transgressions. No one in the room looked pleased as the familiar ceremony got underway:

"Mommy, the Birthday Boy looks scarier than last year!"

"This room is too dark. How are we supposed to take any pictures of the Birthday Boy in here?"

"The Birthday Boy looks like grandma when she died."

"Waaaaahh!"

"No, we can't go home. We just got here!"

"I'm bored."

"Now, Birthday Boy," Denise said slowly, but brightly, "tell the children how you became world-famous for your birthday!"

"I don't remember no more," whimpered Clement as he clasped his shaking hands together and bowed his head.

"Try, Birthday Boy! All the children in the world are just dying to hear your story," Denise gritted as she tried to retain her frozen grin.

Clement tried to muster his energy and courage to remember his lines. "Well, uh, a real long time ago, there were these people, I mean, uh, my parents wanted a baby, but my mother couldn't have no kids, but then my father knocked her up when she was too old to have 'em..."

"Wait a minute," one of the older photographers replied as he strained to get a better look at the old man sitting on the throne. "That doesn't look or sound like Ritchie Ridgley! What kind of colossal joke are you people trying to pull?"

"Whatever do you mean?" asked Capshaw nervously.

"I mean that's not the real Birthday Boy! I've been at these birthday parties for twenty years and I know a bad paint job and bad lighting when I see it! What happened to Ritchie Ridgley?"

"You lookin' for the Birthday Boy..?" a faint, but familiar wavering voice asked.

"Who's that, Mommy? He looks scary," one little voice asked in distress.

Everyone turned around and looked at the frail lanky figure standing in the doorway in a wrinkled green polyester suit and bow tie. The old man was trembling and holding his bald head. He looked disheveled and disoriented, but there could be no doubt to the identity: it was Ritchie.

"Look, it's the Birthday Boy!" another child cried as he clung to his mother's leg in fear.

The Birthday Boy squinted his sagging eyes as he studied the sobbing figure sitting on throne. "Clement Gotch, is that you?"

"Yes," wept Clement.

"Whatcha doin' on my throne wearing make-up and boobs?

Before Clement could answer, Denise took the microphone and began to speak in a cheery tone: "Well, boys and girls, look who's here! It's the real Birthday Boy of Bingford just in time to unveil this year's secret theme!"

"Which is?" asked a confused Capshaw.

"I'm glad you asked that question, Mayor Capshaw. The theme of this year's birthday party is 'No other Birthday Boy like it in the world.' We secretly dressed up another man as the Birthday Boy, but you kids were too clever and that's why we brought the real Birthday Boy back. So, even though there may be a lot of birthday boys out there, there will never be a birthday boy quite like the Birthday Boy of Bingford! Everybody, give the Birthday Boy a big round of applause!"

As the confused guests applauded, Denise quickly took a gold paper crown, left the stage, and walked over to the Birthday Boy who was still holding his head.

"I hereby declare you king of all birthdays! Let's all sing a special Happy Birthday to Bingford's most famous birthday boy," she said happily as she placed the paper crown on the Birthday Boy's bald head. She then led Ritchie to his throne where Clement was sitting.

"This is your rightful place, Birthday Boy! Say, kids, let's chase away the fake Birthday Boy!"

With one hand, Denise grabbed Clement by his frail, trembling arm and yanked him off his chair. With her other hand she pulled Ritchie by his arm and pushed him onto the throne. As Clement began to weep anew, a smiling Denise dragged him to one corner of the room while children ran up to hit and kick him on his thighs and shins. When they reached the far end of the room, Denise left him in the corner and returned to the stage.

Within seconds, Capshaw lead the traditional singing of "Happy

Birthday" and Denise coaxed the guests to sing a round of "How old are you now?" for which the Birthday Boy warbled on cue:

"I'm a hundred an' three! I'm a hundred an' three! I'm a hundred an' three-eee, and you're all younger than me!"

The guests were encouraged to applaud, listen to more stories, take their picture with the "real" Birthday Boy, and purchase cake and ice cream. When the guests finally left, Ritchie got up from his throne to stretch his legs. As he looked up, he was surrounded by Denise, Mayor Capshaw, Jared, and Homer. In the corner where Denise left him, Clement was still sobbing.

"What the hell happened, Ritchie?" asked a breathless Capshaw as he readjusted his toupee, "We all thought you were dead!"

"Don't yell," griped Ritchie, "my head's still poundin'."

"What happened?" Denise asked as she glared intensely at the Birthday Boy.

"I got drunk on them Birthday Boy champagne. Yesterday, after Homer left. I couldn't take it no more without my magazines. A man's gotta have somethin' pretty to look at and you won't let me go to the Torpedo Mama. And then, when I thought that I had to go through another birthday party the next day, I guess I drank too much since I passed out or had an out-of-body experience or somethin'. Anyways, when I woke up, I was in some freezer with all these flowers. At first, I thought I died and went to heaven 'cause the flowers smelled so nice and it was cold. But then I didn't think heaven would be so dark or give ya that kind of headache; so then I got up and realized I must be in some freezer. I tried opening the door, but it was closed; so I started pounding and Ms. Herman-Helfer heard me and let me out. I think she put me in that freezer to try an' kill me. I always thought she was up to no good even though she said she had no idea how I wound up in there. Anyways, she wrapped me up in a blanket and made me some hot chocolate to warm up."

"When was this?" asked Denise suspiciously.

"Last night," replied the Birthday Boy dutifully.

"You mean to tell me you've been conscious since yesterday and you didn't even tell us?"

"Don't look at me. Ms. Herman-Helfer wouldn't let me go or even use the phone or nothin'. But, like I said, that's because she's tryin' to kill me. I hadda sleep there, too and this morning she me made me breakfast and talked about somethin' or another about geriatric exploitation all day long. Anyways, just now she had to go to the bathroom; so I snuck out when she wasn't looking and here I am."

Jared studied Ritchie closely. "Are you sure you're feeling fine? Maybe we ought to take you to the doctor's. After all, I wouldn't want anything to happen to my invest... I mean our favorite Birthday Boy."

"I ain't sick and I don't wanna see no doctor. I just got a killer headache is all."

There was a moment of silence as everyone perused the Birthday Boy, making certain he was not in need of medical attention.

"Well, I'm glad that's all worked out. I'm so happy, that I could celebrate all night long!" said a satisfied Capshaw.
He clapped his hands once and went to the back of the room to take a piece of leftover cake from the table.

"Me, too," said a relieved Jared, "I think I'll give that lovely Angelique a call and tell her to get her cute little tush over here to add a little spice to this party."

"Angelique? All right! She's one hot mama! I think I'll stay around to party, too," Homer said as he began to bump and grind to the song he was singing aloud.

Denise shook her head as she took out a cigarillo from her suitcase. "Not until you take Clement back to the nursing home. We don't need him anymore. Now, where's that champagne..."

As Homer took a weeping Clement outside, Ritchie looked around in disgust and shook a defiant fist in the air.

"Not another celebration! I'm gettin' sick of all these birthday parties. It's always the same old thing! If it ain't a bunch of rotten smelly l'il kids whinin' and cryin' and peein' themselves, it's a bunch of bossy grown ups tellin' me what to do. I hate birthdays, 'specially my own. Make me sick," he grumbled as he sat on his red-and-gold colored throne. He took off his gold-colored paper crown and tore it to shreds.

Lance and Bunny

I

She: an innocuously gullible woman; not much for conversation, unless you count the four hours a day she talked to her Lancie and the three hours a day she spent moralizing and gossiping with her mother on the phone – never mind the fact her mother legally disowned her only daughter five years ago.

He: a belligerent, lanky fellow who lacked an appetite and a functioning sense of humor. He was a supposed anti-intellectual who possessed a graduate degree in psychology; psychoacoustics to be precise. Yet, he felt no sense of joy since he knew the secrets he unearthed, mainly first-year student subjects tend to lie a lot, weren't applicable to the real world.

They: a murky, slightly eccentric combination of Urban Myth Believer and Paranoid Conspiracy Theorist. Whatever you said about them – you knew she'd almost always believe everything she heard and he'd believe almost nothing he ever read.

II

"Lancie?"

"What now, Bunny?"

"Why can't we have fun like all the other couples?"

He grimaced. He knew what was coming next. In emotionally manipulative times like these, Lance knew the best line of defense was a good dose of deconstructionism and denial. It was time for his brand of steely stealth.

He attacked firmly, but casually. "Get with the times, Bunny – it's politically incorrect to have fun. Monotony is in – it offends no one."

"That's not true!" She pouted with conviction. The gentle May breeze cooled and dried her sulky lower lip. She sipped her lemonade to remoisten her mouth.

"Look at that couple over there," she pointed, directing her love to the absorbed young couple who were kissing each other's giggling lips in the bus shelter.

"See?" Bunny reiterated, "They're having fun. We should do that."

"We do that," he protested underneath his grim cloud. He sipped his beer as he flicked an ant off the sticky table. He hoped the waiter would come outside to the patio and give him the bill.

"We don't do enough of that. Not in public. You don't show people you love me."

"Don't be ridiculous! You think that's love?" he gritted as he waved his hand at the bus shelter couple, "That's not love! That's bragging. I don't believe in bragging."

"That's not bragging. That's fun."

So her argument came full circle, he grumbled in his thoughts. Fun. Fun. Fun. Those two exhibitionists weren't having fun. They were pretending to have fun. If one was sharp and adept enough, one could deduce these things. As a heuristic, overtly lusting couples were never in love. Or lust. To these people, heavy petting in public was a cover. Those actions could only mean one thing – private screaming matches known to no one but the old widower neighbor who was forced to listen to the sordid wailing and smashing glass at the most inconvenient hours.

Lance knew what that meant – the open displays, the man or the woman – was marking his (her?) territory. "Don't touch; this is mine." Maybe that's what the screaming at night was about: wayward genitals and an untrue heart. Possible. Lance hoped the bus would soon come and quickly sweep the offending couple from his world.

"Lancie! Didn't you hear a word I said?" Bunny yelled.

"Obviously not. Say it again."

"I said, 'We never have fun anymore.' Look around you! It's spring! Everyone's..."

Lance tuned out Bunny. That naif was at it again. She was always taking appearances at face value. If every girl on the block ran around with a panting, leering Lothario, then, by gum, Bunny had to run around with one, too.

He furrowed and molded his pale face until he obtained the right degree of indignation and annoyance.

"I don't want to talk about this anymore. You're so naive, Bunny. Why do you keep insisting on this nonsense? What's with you today?"

Bunny revisited her pout. She looked angry.

"Lance! We're in a public place! Keep it down!"

"Only if you tell me what's with this 'make-out-in-public' kick of yours."

"Shhh! People will hear you."

This was Bunny's fuzzy logic: it was all right to simulate sexual intercourse in public, but shouting about the act was vulgar.

She quieted down as she nestled in her seat, getting ready to reveal the reason behind her new concern. She took a deep breath. She was ready.

"I was talking to my mother today and she told me Sarah-Ann DeMasco and her boyfriend…"

Lance rolled his eyes as his nerves began to fray and he immersed in a sense of dread.

"…and she said the two of them are so much in love. They go bowling and minigolfing and they do all sorts of fun things together. Not like us! We never go anywhere and we never have any fun."

Besides the absurdity and contradictions in her remarks, Bunny sounded jealous. No, she was envious. It was an envy based on lies. Lance scrunched his lips as he raised his nearly invisible eyebrow.

"What do you mean I never take you anywhere? We're in a restaurant, are we not? And you think minigolf is more romantic than food? You need to see a more qualified therapist than the one you have now!"

"There is nothing wrong with Dr. Slater. He really helped me after that disowning thing with my mom. You should go see him, Lancie."

"And do you really believe anything Sarah-Ann DeMasco says? Grow up! She's just trying to make you envy her. I cannot believe how utterly naive you are."

"I am not!"

"You are. Remember when Wallace Crumb and Bud Augley convinced you that there were such things as goat eggs?"

Bunny winced, angry at Lance's infallible memory and his cruel use of it. "Do I have to pay for that mistake for the rest of my life?"

"I never trusted Wallace," Lance continued, his thoughts shielding him from Bunny's current tirade. "He was always such a malevolent character. I don't care what anybody says, I don't think he actually graduated from that co-op university at all. It was a three-year program and he supposedly graduated five years after enrolling. Even if it was a co-op university – it shouldn't have taken that long. He was always such a braggart, yet, where was his diploma in his apartment? He didn't frame it or show it to

73

anyone and if anyone ever asked him about it, he'd change the subject"

"Lancie! What are you talking about now? Pay attention to me!"

Lance made a face as he looked at Bunny. But all he saw was her pout. How could one woman be so naive and indignant at the same time?

"Well, look who's here! Lance O'Boyle and his little Bunny girl!"

Both Lance and Bunny turned around. Bunny perked up while Lance slumped at the identical stimulus. It was Apricot Leeves – Bunny's ideal woman and Lance's ideal target of torment.

Apricot was not as well-educated as she appeared. Though she behaved as if she had reached the upper echelons of post-secondary education, Apricot had only lasted a single semester at a posh university whose Chancellor was close friends with her father. She was the mistress of masking her flaws with her in-flated ego. And why shouldn't it be inflated? She was the daughter of a very wealthy, very indulging and very well-connected power couple. Apricot had no reason to earn anything: respect, a career, or a diploma – all Miss Leeves had to do was ask Mumzie or Pah-pah for that very special something and that something would arrive at her doorstep instantly.

Her nepotistic gift made up for all her other deficiencies: she was not attractive or shapely, though she carried herself well in her designer clothes which hung on her Pilates-sculpted frame; she was not kind, though her lineage gave her the right kind of friends and lovers without the effort, and she was not diligent, though with her parents' bank accounts and circle of affluent friends, no one really cared that the youngest Leeves had bought into her own hype. What Apricot saw in the mirror every morning, was the most stunningly beautiful, wonderful package who was deserving of everything she received.

Everyone could easily ignore the true nature of her success – except Lance.

Lance could see it all: the flaws, the facade, and the delusions. He had always wondered what Apricot would do if her parents suddenly disowned her, or lost their fortune and became pariahs. But with Apricot's preternaturally good fortune, he knew that would never happen.

"Lancie! Apricot just asked you a very important question. I'm sooooo sorry, Apricot, but Lance has been like this all day long," Bunny alternated between shrilling and groveling. She did not want to displease Apricot, though she failed to notice her idol's state of perpetual indifference.

Apricot shrugged. "Lance isn't the brightest bulb around."

The remark got Lance's attention. "There is nothing deficient in the wattage of my bulb, as you put it. I simply turn if off in your presence because I do not care to waste my energy on the likes of you."

"Lancie!" Bunny shrieked.

Apricot stared unaffectedly at Lance. "I guess when you don't have much to spare, you have to save it anyway you can. So, I guess the two of you won't be coming to my party."

"Of course we will, Apricot! It would be such an honor!" Honour. The word felt like a thick, syrupy poison engulfing

Lance. He fired his distrustful glance at the party giver.

"What party? Why would you invite us to any party? Why would we go?"

"It's to celebrate my cover spread. Apricot Leeves on the cover of Haute. It's going to be the first of many, but any excuse to throw a party."

Apricot landing on the cover of Haute could hardly be surprising since the arrogant and anorexic editrix was her godmother. An aspiring model who had a gangly leg up in her career sickened him. Lance thought to himself he would throw a party, too, if his godmother were the editor of the Journal of Psychology.

Bunny became excited for Apricot. "Oh, I am so excited for you, Apricot. Not everyone can get on the cover of Haute!"

"No, it's not easy," conceded Apricot, "they only put the prettiest and slimmest girls on their covers. You can't sell fashion magazines any other way. Someone has to make the clothes look good." She became a little more irritated and demanding, "Are you coming or not?"

"Yeah, right," scoffed Lance.

"Of course we will! What time should we come?" cooed Bunny.

Lance wished Bunny wouldn't feed into Apricot's ego. Bunny wished Lance wouldn't be so cruel to Apricot. Apricot smiled serenely – two more guests on her list.

III

A party. A fancy party. A fancy party hosted by a fashion model. A fancy party hosted by a fashion model who happened to be her friend. Oh, the joys of life! Bunny was so excited that she could barely coat her toenails with polish without going over. She could hardly believe her luck. Apricot never invited her to any of her parties. But then again, Apricot was never on the cover of Haute.

Haute was such a great magazine. It was big and thick and had a lot of ads from the biggest fashion houses in the world. What to wear, where to shop, what lip-gloss to use and how to use it to maximize the woman in you. Then there were all those informative articles on what to say to your boyfriend and what lingerie to wear to maximize the man in him (though they never seemed to work on Lancie). There were celebrity interviews, those monthly self-awareness quizzes and, of course, Segna Turnbull's numerology column that always seemed to be so dead-on, even if Lancie complained the entries were so vague and silly they would even apply to Bunny's dog Sasha. Lancie could never admit he was wrong.
Apricot on the cover of Haute. That was an ostrich plume in her cap.

Bunny's excitement was cut short by the knocking at her door. Lancie here already? But she hadn't even put on her new dress yet. She took a quick look in the mirror before she answered her apartment door – her long, fuzzy, brown hair cascaded in all the right ways and her make-up looked dramatic, yet fresh and crisp.

"Lancie! What are you doing here?"

Lance rolled his bulging eyes as he groaned. "Why do you think I'm here? I came to pick you up to take you to this sorry excuse for a party. You aren't even dressed yet, and we are running late as it is."

"Lancie! We don't want to get there too early. But I'm so excited! I can't wait to go! I never get invited to Apricot's parties! Give me a minute. I'll put on my new dress. Don't go anywhere; just wait right there."

Bunny leaped into the bedroom and slammed the door behind her as she giggled happily. Lance leaned his lanky frame against the door. He could hear Bunny rustling in the bedroom, bumping into furniture, tripping over her feet, zipping up her dress.

A few moments later, she burst open the bedroom door dramatically and giddily tumbled into the living room, where Lance was impatiently waiting.

"Well? What do you think? Don't I look fancy, Lancie?"

What was there for Lance to say? Bunny had been partially devoured by a monstrous pink gown – her head and glittered bare shoulders barely peered out from under the large, puffy, neon-pink lace and organza. The long, bloated train made Bunny's derriere look five times its regular size. It was the largest, ugliest, and most hideous dress Lance had ever seen.

"What on earth is that monstrosity you're wearing? Is this some kind of sick joke?"

"Lancie!"

"What possessed you to ... to buy that wretched, overgrown piece of stale cotton candy? Bunny, you ought to be ashamed!"

Bunny almost began to cry. "The saleslady said I looked very pretty in this evening dress."

"That is not an evening dress! That is a wedding gown for a tacky serial bride. I cannot believe that you let yourself get talked into purchasing that outdated outfit! The sales- lady is a scam artist who unloaded that decade-old dress on you."

"Lancie! How could you say something like that. This is a fancy party. I have to wear a fancy dress."

"For the last time, that is not a dress, that is a wedding gown! You let yourself get swindled by a simple sales- woman. Those people will say just about anything to make a sale."

Bunny began to pout. How could Lancie be so insensitive? His outfit was an embarrassment, not hers: black loose- fitting slacks, a ratty black turtleneck sweater, and an old brown jacket. It was as if he didn't care to go to Apricot's party. He had no under- standing of the importance of wearing nice clothes to a nice party.

It was no use. She took her bubble gum-pink purse and wore her matching pink sandals, and opened the door. How was she go- ing to explain to Apricot why Lance wasn't dressed very nicely for a very important party?

As they walked to Lance's car, Bunny tugged at his jacket and stopped walking.

"Before we get inside your car, Lancie, you better check under it."

"Why? Do you see an oil leak?"

"Not that! Daffodil told me that she heard that some robbers hide under cars and then cut women's ankles with a knife. Can you imagine that, Lancie? Isn't that terrible?"

"You have nothing to worry about," gritted an annoyed Lance, "with that dress, no robber will be able to find your ankles; he most likely will end up getting tangled in that inflated beach ball you're wearing. Let's go."

IV

The steady tide of urbane laughter and sophisticated conversation told Apricot that she had triumphed once again as the party hostess without peer. She made sure the hors d'oeuvres were delectable, yet accessible to the weight conscious. The music was tasteful enough for all to enjoy as were the liqueurs. Apricot's hair and make-up were done up to enhance her unquestionable radiance. Her sleek black dress was becoming of a blossoming fashion model. Sheer elegance and understatement was the law of the Leeves and so far, Apricot's instincts were impeccable as usual.

Everything would be perfect. It was already coming together as she had meticulously planned: most of the guests had already eagerly arrived on time; everyone had oohed and aahed with conviction over her high profile coup. The guests were revolving around her, congratulating her on her first magazine cover. Another resounding success was within her dainty grasp.

Just as Misty Hayes had begun to compare Apricot's flawless porcelain complexion to that of an Oscar-winning A-list actress, the doorbell rang. Apricot opened the door, then blanched in horror. It took every ounce of willpower for her not to scream or weep. Her dreams of a perfect party were hopelessly shattered. In front of her blueberry-sweet eyes were a ridiculously lanky slob of a man dressed as a disheveled hobo and a woman in a hideous pink wedding gown. Lance and Bunny.

"I think you two were mistaken," heaved a noticeably upset Apricot, "This wasn't a costume party!"

"I know that, Apricot. Don't you like my new dress? I bought it just for this party."

Lance grimaced. "Well, Apricot? Aren't you going to let us in to get this alleged party over and done with? Heaven only knows why you invited us here."

"Lancie! Don't be so rude! I am sooooo sorry, Apricot. I don't know what's gotten into him. He was rude to me, too! Can you believe he didn't like my new dress?"

How dare they? How dare they ruin her perfect party? How dare they steal the limelight from her on her big night? Apricot had extended a courtesy and in return those two made it seem as if she cavorted with common folk. It was unbearable and galling. Bunny never wore such a ridiculous outfit before. Granted, her clothes were always bordering on passé and common, but never garish. Lance never wore clothes so raggedy before. It was obvious: Lance and his girlfriend had deliberately set out to destroy her party. At the very least, Lance had coerced Bunny into participating in an act of deliberate and methodical sabotage. But what could she do to salvage her big night?

It was obvious Apricot was too busy gawking at Bunny's monstrosity to let her two guests into her home. Lance pushed himself and Bunny past the ungracious Miss Leeves into the living room.

Lance groaned at the sight of his fellow invitees. The guests were repulsive enough to warrant access into Apricot's home, he thought as he scrunched his lips. Wallace, Misty, Charity, and Bud were the most suspicious of the bunch. Misty was a shameless kiss-up who would lick just about any set of filthy boots if it meant climbing one rung higher on the social ladder. Charity Case was a shameless exaggerator and prevaricator whose only purpose in life was to make others jealous of her ersatz success. Bud and Wallace could not be trusted on any account: they had already beguiled Bunny on numerous occasions just for their own sick amusement. But most galling of all the guests was Ross.

82

C. Ross Rhodes. The name itself made Lance swell and boil with fury. The pretentious lout, who he was convinced was the owner of numerous salacious and closeted secrets, had always made the debutantes and the gold diggers swelter, swoon and swivel in his presence. Apricot's perfect boyfriend relished this power – he would smile and flirt for his adoring audience. Rhodes had all the right features for his part: thirty-two perfect white teeth; a head of thick wavy brown hair; the dimply smile; the rippling, well-tended muscles and flawless flesh that stacked up to six feet, four inches, and that didn't include his bullish bank account, or his enviable career as a stock broker.

The snatches of conversation had suddenly ceased.

"Hi everyone," Bunny chirped. "Are you as excited as Lancie and I are?"

"Speak for yourself," Lance interjected grimly.

"Bunny! Look at your dress!" Misty spluttered.

"Thank you. When I saw it in the window, I knew it was the perfect dress for Apricot's party."

"Isn't it a little ... big?" Charity asked awkwardly, failing to find the right words.

"No, it's the right size. It doesn't feel loose at all," Bunny replied.

Lance grabbed a champagne glass from a waiter's tray and downed it in one gulp. This was going to be a long night.

V

After one long, slow, life-draining hour, Apricot's preposterous and pretentious party was still in full swing. The conversation was a nonstop mockery of human interaction, thought Lance as he endured sixty full minutes of deceit, shallowness, and self-indulgent vaunting. At the moment, the main focus of the party was at the instant pictures taken during Apricot's photo shoot.

"Apricot, you look so gorgeous in these photos," gushed Misty as she pawed and drooled over the pictures.

"It's so true!" Bunny agreed unfeigned as she nodded her head.

Apricot was just about to agree with Misty, when Lance grimaced as he looked at the two-faced gusher. "Really, Misty? Is that why you told Daffodil Meadows that Apricot had a horse's head?"

Misty slunk back in her chair, looking fearfully at a steaming Apricot. "Uh, umm..."

"Charity," asked Wallace between sips of his drink, "what's up with you? Last I heard, you left your publicist's position at Bates and Wilson."

Charity straightened her back as she replied proudly, "I got a new job. Seventy-five thousand dollars a year, stock options, company car..."

Bunny's eyes widened. "Charity! That is great! Congratulations."

Lance arched his invisible eyebrow at a beaming Charity. "Given your modest background, where did you find such an incredible position? You haven't been working as a publicist for more than a year."

Charity became antsy. "Well, it's a small company downtown. You probably, ah, haven't heard of it."

Lance persisted. "Nonsense. I like to keep abreast of the city's smaller enterprises. What does this small company do?"

"I don't know, " Charity muttered nervously. She sunk into her seat and fumbled with her dress.

"Don't know? How very interesting. I suppose, you don't know what position you fill there, either..."

"Well, everyone," Ross interrupted as he nonchalantly and suavely acknowledged all his fellow party revelers with his mes- merizing, studied glance while lightly tossing Apricot's proofs on the glass coffee table in front of him, "I think we should keep the conversation a little lighter..."

With a well-timed giggle and a practiced scrunch of her ski jump nose, Misty regained her composure and patted Ross's sturdy left arm as she cooed, "You always know what's best, Rossy."

Not wanting to miss the chance to drool and fawn over Apricot's most attractive fashion accessory, Charity rubbed Ross's right shoulder as she nodded greedily, "Oh, he sure does! So, Rossy, what's new with you? Still making a bundle on the market?"

"Well, yes," Ross replied thoughtfully, "it's a bullish market this season and with my expertise, I have managed to do quite well for myself."

"That is because the public is easy to swindle and manipulate, no doubt..," Lance interjected.

"Lancie, this is a party! Why aren't we having fun?" Bunny

pouted as she fluffed up her dress. "I talked to my mother on the phone today and she said Sarah-Ann DeMasco and her boy-friend just had a party and everyone had fun there. They were playing charades and twister and everything. They weren't talk-ing about the stock market and that boring stuff!"

"Thank you, Bunny," Lance blurted curtly. "It was your idea to come here in the first place. I told you no good would come of it. Is that why you insisted we come to this farce – because Sarah-Ann DeMasco had a party?"

"Of course not. Why are you so mad?"

"Because this party is a waste of time!"

"That's because you keep interrupting and saying really rude things, Lance."

"I am merely uncovering certain truths."

"It's quite all right, Bunny," Ross replied soothingly as he took a sip from his drink, "I rather enjoy friendly, if rigorous debates. It livens up the evening. So, Lance, you think I am a common con man?"

"Nothing about you is common, Ross," Lance conceded as he began on a fresh glass of spirits. "If you were, then you would not be driving an expensive car or wearing that ridiculously ex-pensive suit. Your schemes to fleece the greedy and the desper-ate are on a grander scale..."

"Lancie, stop it; you're ruining everything," pleaded Bunny, des-perately trying to salvage the evening.

As Bunny's whining became shriller and Apricot's face became more pallid, Wallace and Bud, who had both been deliberately trying to blend in with the wallpaper, began to stir. Now that the party was a total write-off, they looked at each other with devilish glee. There was only one way to rescue this dud of a vanity soirée: by having a little fun at Bunny's expense. Wallace perked up as he looked at his pigeon. "Say, Bunny, have you been on the balcony here? The view's just fabulous! Come on; Bud and I will show you."

Bunny perked up and with an effortless hop managed to get up from the couch, a large pink cloud behind her. "Oh, I would love to see it, Wallace. I'm coming!"

"Bunny, watch yourself," Lance warned sternly, while hurling a distrustful glance and Wallace and Bud.

"Lancie, stop it," Bunny dismissed as she bounced behind a bemused twosome.

The three had not been on the balcony more than a minute when Wallace turned to look at Bunny.

"You know, Bunny, after seeing you in that dress of yours, I think you're wasting your time with Lance. If you were to talk to Apricot, I bet she'd see to it that you got the next cover of Haute," he stated with an obnoxious smirk.

Bunny looked at a snickering Wallace and Bud with her widened brown eyes. "Really?"

"Of course," chimed Bud, trying hard not to burst into a fit of hysterical laughter. "With your fashion sense, Bunny, I can't imagine anyone turning you down."

Bunny beamed with pride while she lifted and flounced her

dress. "You think I should ask Apricot if I could be on the cover of Haute?"

"Yes, Bunny. I was just remarking to Bud how no one I've ever met can dress like you. Why don't you ask Apricot if her godmother wouldn't mind putting you on the cover – with that dress. When the world sees what a bastion of elegance you are, there's no telling..."

At this chicanery, Lance became enraged and burst out onto the balcony. "Wallace, you miserable excuse for a man, stop trying to bamboozle Bunny!"

"But, Lancie, Wallace was just saying that..."

"Yes, I heard what that decrepit and malicious scoundrel told you. Crumb, you ought to be ashamed of yourself!"

"Now, now, Lance," Wallace replied coolly, "I have no idea what you're getting at..."

"Goat's eggs, that's what! Now, you either come clean to Bunny or I will personally hurl you two over that balcony."

"Lancie!"

Wallace looked at the lanky Lance: even though that wiry cynic was outnumbered two to one, he knew Lance was angry and eccentric enough to carry out his deranged threat.

"All right," ceded a chortling and unrepentant Crumb, "Bud and I were just having a little fun with you, Bunny."
Bunny became so deflated that even her dress drooped. "Wallace! Why do you have to be so mean?"

"Ah, come on, Bunny," Bud snickered, trying halfheartedly to appear good-natured and not vicious. "Lighten up. We didn't mean any harm."

"You meant nothing *but* harm to Bunny! Get out of here, you two scoundrels!"

Wallace and Bud departed amid a stream of stifled laughs and unconvincing coughs.

Lance rolled his eyes and shook his head.

"The problem with you, Bunny, is that you fall for everything!"

"I do not!"

"What about now?"

"Why wouldn't I believe them? They said I had a pretty dress on. I think it's a pretty dress, Misty and Charity thought it was a pretty dress, even the lady at the store said so. Why would they sell ugly dresses and then charge lots of money for them?"

"I've had enough of this nonsense. Let's go!"

"But, Lancie, we haven't even been here for a couple of hours!"

"Even that's too long. Come on."

Lance gently took Bunny by her small, cold hand and escorted his love into Apricot's living room.

"We must be going now, Apricot," Lance declared sternly as he lead a squirming and reluctant Bunny to the front hall.

Apricot looked disappointed as she softly put her hand on Lance's shoulder. At this gesture, he stopped and studied the disheartened hostess.

"Leaving so soon? I was hoping you'd stay a little longer. You just got here."

"Why do you care? I'm sure you will be more than happy to be rid of us, and the sentiment, I assure you, is mutual."

"Lance," Apricot said sweetly, "I don't feel that way. I invited you and Bunny to my party because I wanted to celebrate with all my friends. I know what happened on the balcony, but Wallace and Bud are just a couple of jokers. I don't think that's a reason to leave so early. Please stay."

Before Lance had a chance to analyze and evaluate Apricot's olive branch offer for flaws, he glanced over at Bunny; she didn't seem overly moved by Apricot's plea.

"Come on, Lancie. Let's go. I don't want to stay; we haven't played even *one* game of charades! We're not having any fun here."

"A few seconds ago, you didn't want to leave."

"I know, but I'm getting bored now. Let's go and do something fun together."

"Oh, let them go, Apricot," Wallace snapped after swallowing a mouthful of beggar's purse. "They're just a couple of killjoys, anyway. They've got no sense of humor."

"Wallace, that's enough," Apricot stated firmly.

The turn of events was perplexing. If this were some scam, then Wallace most certainly would have wanted both Bunny and him to stay. On the other hand, if they defy Apricot's request, it may be all part of some nefarious plan. Lance looked around the room for signs: Misty, Charity, and Bud were sitting on the plush white sofa, looking curiously at him. Ross was still drinking his scotch, looking utterly disinterested at the entire scene.

"Hmmm, " Lance finally said after some thought. "All right, we'll stay a little while longer, if you wish."

"Thank you, Lance," Apricot said serenely as she rotated a large, gold bracelet on her dainty wrist.

Lance nodded while Bunny looked confused. After she scrunched her nose for a few seconds, she whispered in Lance's ear: "You really want to stay, Lance? But I thought you hated Apricot. Are you sure you don't want to go and fun somewhere else? We're not having any fun here."

Lance whispered back, "You are obsessed with fun! What's with you?"

"Lancie, I didn't get dressed up to be unhappy!"

As Lance and Bunny were debating about Bunny's mood swings in ghost tones, both failed to notice that Apricot had disappeared from the living room.

"Where did Apricot go, Ross?" asked Misty, looking over her shoulder.
Ross shrugged as he looked at his gold watch. "I have no idea. It's getting rather late and I have an early morning meeting tomorrow with an important client. She's rather difficult to please, but with my charms, I usually can persuade her; that is, if I get

my eight hours of beauty sleep."
"If Apricot doesn't come back in a couple of minutes, I'm leaving," yawned Wallace.

"Me, too," nodded Bud and stretched his stocky legs.

"I have to get to work early tomorrow," noted Charity as she looked over Lance sternly.

In a few minutes, Apricot emerged from her bedroom with a large stack of photographs and a small black pouch wedged between her arm and her side. She smelled of freshly sprayed perfume and her hair and make-up looked as glowing as it did two hours ago. She had obviously gone to her bedroom to touch up her flaws, noted Lance. He frowned at the new torturous mound of pictures. No wonder she had wanted both he and Bunny to remain at the party.

"I brought some more pictures from some of my other shoots for us to look over," said Apricot nonchalantly as she placed them carefully on the coffee table. Misty looked intensely at both the photos and the pouch.

"What's in the bag, Apricot?" she finally asked as Apricot placed the pictures in smaller piles on the table.

"This?" Apricot shrugged and calmly took the black pouch, and opened it to reveal an expensive camera. "I just wanted to take a few pictures of my friends to cherish the memories." She took the camera and gave it to Wallace. "Would you be so kind as to take a few photos of me and Misty, Wallace?"

"Sure, Apricot," complied Wallace and docilely obeyed her request. Within moments, he had taken pictures of Apricot with Misty, Charity, and Ross, with Apricot always striking a casual, but calculated model's pose, while openly fussing about lighting and camera angles. She then asked Charity to take a few pictures of her with Wallace and Bud; then took the camera from Charity and asked various groupings of friends to stand or sit together for group shots. Finally, she turned to Lance and Bunny. "I'd like to take a couple of pictures of the two of you, too. Do you mind?"

"I'd rather not," Lance begged off.

"Lancie! Don't be mean! We can have our picture taken if Apricot wants," Bunny insisted, while fixing her flowing locks.

Apricot took the same care with lighting and posing when she posed and photographed a slouching and vexed Lance and a perky and compliant Bunny. When she was satisfied with her handiwork, she nodded.

"Yes," she said somewhat curtly, "that will do." She paused. "By the way, Bunny, Wallace and Bud told me what they said to you on the balcony, about how you ought to be in a fashion magazine. I thought about their little joke, and you know what?"

"What?" Bunny asked eagerly.

"You and Lance will be in Haute after all."

Bunny looked surprised. "Really?"

"Really," Apricot replied with a petty, diabolical stare. At this, Lance stood up straight.

"What are you getting at?" he asked suspiciously.

"I told you: you and Bunny will be in next edition of Haute. I am going to make sure of it. There is a perfect section in the magazine for you two."

Bunny's wide eyes shone radiantly. "Where's that? The 'about town' section?"

"No, no," Apricot purred as she sauntered over to the front door, "it's better than that. It's going to be put in the 'jokes of fashion' section. You know, the one where all the real life fashion blunders are displayed for the world to see and snicker at?"

"What!?" Bunny spluttered. "Apricot! You're joking!"

"Absolutely not," Apricot spat as she opened her front door. "Now leave!"

"How dare you pull this cruel and ghastly stunt on Bunny? She's done nothing to you, you ugly and wicked spoiled brat," Lance growled as he took Bunny by the arm and walked outside.

Apricot's face contorted in a red fury as she screamed, "How *dare* she try to upstage me at my own party and ruin everything. How *dare* you come here dressed like a beggar and belittle my friends. I have never been so insulted. Instead of being grateful I let you two into my home, you just bluster in late, insult my friends, and show brazen disrespect to your betters! I only invited you two because Daffodil and her boyfriend couldn't make it!" Apricot hissed at Bunny. "I never want to see you two again. How *dare* you ruin my party."

It took Lance a minute to realize what happened. In a daze, he stomped to his car, oblivious that Bunny was not behind him. In the seconds between shock and comprehension, he felt his nerves scream and shake: Apricot had outwitted him by striking at him through Bunny.

94

How could he have fallen for such a sophomoric ploy played by a shallow dilettante such as Apricot? Of course, she wanted Bunny and him to stay: how could she mete out her punishment if they left? He could not believe he was that naive. The unspeakable had happened: he had been duped by a lesser intellect. He was speechless.

Apricot slammed the door to return to her fawning guests. She would not pay for this evening's sins. Not now. Not ever.

Lance considered his options.

The most obvious and instinctually gratifying solution was to kill her or maim her. But he would most likely miss, get arrested, be demonized and labeled as an envious misogynist by the press and spend the rest of his productive years in prison, while Apricot would be seen as a good person and worse, a martyr. A book deal and movie-of-the-week would be a certainty. Her win would be cemented the in the glossy magazines she adored.

Lance considered various scenarios of plots and schemes to exact his revenge. Even if all conditions were ideal, every route would ultimately lead to a Leeves conquest. He sighed and decided: Apricot was not worth another atom of his energy or attention. He would not nourish her cancerous ego by allowing himself to give her a second thought, while she shrugged him off, or bragged about his narrow focus to her sycophant friends. If he obsessed, he would prolong her victory. He would not give her that satisfaction. She had not earned his attention and, for once, she would not bypass her dues to get what she wanted. Whether his inattention ate at her or was beneath her notice, so be it, he thought. Whatever her fate in life, it was no longer a concern to him. Not now. Not ever.

"Lancie! Lancie, where are you?"

"Right here," he muttered, ashamed.

Bunny tripped forward in her bloated cotton candy dress until she came face to face with him. He looked at her: Bunny looked visibly angry, but even in all her ire, she looked sympathetically at him. Had she turned against him? Was she pitying him? For once, Lance could not anchor himself or provide a plausible theory.

Bunny broke the silence. "Oh, Lancie, I'm so sorry."

"It's my fault, Bunny; I should have known better than to believe anything Apricot says."

"It's not your fault. It doesn't really matter, anyway. I mean, it's not all that great to be humiliated in front of so many people at a fancy party and then in a magazine, but it's a lot better than that disowning thing with my mom. I'm just sorry you got hurt, too, Lancie. But, I'll tell you one thing: I'm never buying Haute again if they put people like Apricot on the cover."

Lance looked up at her and smiled. "So you don't blame me."

Bunny scrunched her nose as she looked tenderly at him. "Of course not. Apricot was mean and rude. She makes me so mad! But, I feel sorry for her anyway. Ross didn't even look at her once the whole time. No wonder. She can keep her boring parties and all her fake friends. I don't care about her anymore. Let's have our own fun."

"After everything that transpired here tonight? You still want to go out?"

"Do you know how much I paid for this dress, Lancie? I want to get some fun out of it ... before I burn it. Let's go mini-golfing."

Lance bulged his disbelieving eyes at Bunny. "In that dress ...
um, all right, the night's still young. I owe you one."

Bunny jumped up and kissed her Lancie on the nose. "You are
so great! We're going to have some real fun now. I'm so excited I
can't wait! I love you, Lancie."

Lance held Bunny close to his chest. He closed his eyes as did
she. There was silence, but no words were needed. Nothing else
mattered. There was nothing in this universe to be pondered,
analyzed, constructed, deconstructed, ameliorated, exposed, de-
bated. The answer was resting on his chest. No matter how
many mistaken beliefs she held, no matter how many missteps
she took in the past – he knew she was above all else his best
friend and she would never steer him wrong.

In his overstuffed, tentacled mind, he knew he had a lot of catching up to do.

Wain in Vain

I

Art wasn't just a language or a yardstick for cultural intelligence; it was also something to gawk at on weekday afternoons. The museum was an uncharacteristically busy hub for the hip and chic today; the elongated and meandering stretches of clean, cool, white space were studiously littered with imposing and epic paintings and sculptures along with their curious admirers. Each large and small corner had its own clique of artwork, all competing for attention and plaudits for their creators. A bantam exhibit of delicate and lithe Japanese dolls shyly graced a small room to the left; a flamboyant cadre of rollicking and ribald, beaded, surrealist sculptures flashed their proud, fragmented selves to the right. The requisite collection of veteran oil paintings stood patiently as both young and old eyes gazed upon their seasoned beauty.

Yet, none of these works would dare compete with the large and dynamic crowd congregating excitedly by the cordoned-off main room. For whatever reason, the star attraction did not wish to see its aroused visitants until show time. Though access was haughtily denied, the coldness did not damper the growing and glowing crowd of chatty bystanders.

Usually, this city's museum was the metropolis' best-kept secret, especially on this type of cold, unforgiving January evening. To-day, attendance was strangely large and boisterous, even when the patrons were whispering and speculating about the exhibit they came to see – yet none of this crowd seemed to be regular connoisseurs of the arts. Journalists were present, chatting away nervously on their cells phones. Young adults who proclaimed allegiance to various underground and pseudo-underground schools of fashion, made the time to grace the museum with their hipper-than-thou presence. Well-heeled fashionistas and their dandy companions choreographed their posing and preen-ing as they waited for their sanctioned stimulation. For most of those waiting for their amusements, it was an odd trek to make in the first place, many seemed unsure of how to get to the ex-hibit du jour.

Not all patrons were concerning themselves with the chattering, patchwork mob. There was one - a tall, dignified, and well-dressed man in his fifties - whose glances and wanderings be-trayed his interest in almost every work in the building. Though he had popped into the museum to briefly shelter from the vi-cious elements, it was a welcome refuge from his preternaturally hectic life. The impromptu visit brought him back to those more laid-back days, when he could take advantage of the university's art museum between classes and fondly recall his art history elective. His current diversion had been a welcome, but bitter-sweet one.

As usual, his time was limited: which exhibit should he savor before going back to devour his competitors? The Japanese dolls were stunning, and he had entertained the idea to purchase the one that reminded him of his lovely, sweet daughter who was at the moment settling into her second semester at university. He rejected the exhibit on the grounds that the temptation to make an expensive, impulsive buy based on sentimental notions would probably not go over well with his new wife.

The beaded, surrealist sculptures were also rejected on the grounds that standing next to too much purple, orange, and green was not becoming of a newly minted vice president of a multinational corporation; however, standing next to old paintings would make him look too stodgy and timid. After a few seconds of strategic browsing, he opted to look at a group of large abstract clay sculptures next to the main room.

As soon as he entered the room, the man looked at the works and nodded his head in approval: good luck was on his side after all. Not only were the sculptures a safe and image-friendly choice, but the pieces were a fluid and elegant chorus that almost seemed to in unison serenade him the importance of bravery, inner peace and kindness toward your fellow man. Though the creator was long dead, her convictions and her voice lived on in her work, the man thought pensively as he slowly walked around each sculpture, trying to absorb the tranquility emanating from each work. It reminded him of his first wife's own painful battle that she finally lost in a hospital bed, and how his young daughter stood by him in their time of grief. The porcelain doll he had seen earlier brought back memories of his only child's stoic grace at her mother's deathbed. Though the man had gotten far in his career on his uncanny ability to read the thoughts of others; there was satisfaction in knowing he could read and share those same thoughts in a symbolic way.

"Well? Don't just stand there. Tell me, what do you make of this piece?" a demanding and terse female voice abruptly asked. The man seemed startled as his melancholy thoughts were overpowered by the loud, impudent question. He quickly looked around as he heard the same low, disembodied voice insist, "Go on. I'd love to hear what you think of all this."

The man soon found the source of the proud, commanding voice. The gaunt, toned young woman could not be older than twenty-five, though her husky speech sounded at least twenty years older than her unlined face. Though she could not be classified as "unattractive," there was something decidedly singular and upsetting about her appearance and demeanor. She was a tall woman; at least six feet without her stiletto heels. She was blonde and blue-eyed with long eyelashes, though it was obvious that the hue of her eyes wasn't truly blue, the long lashes weren't hers, and the exceedingly long roll of blonde hair wasn't truly blonde – in fact, her mane seemed to be nothing more than bleached hair extensions. Her fingernails looked well-tended, if acrylic. Even the material of her full, ample breasts was suspect, as were the original shape of her ski jump nose and high cheekbones; however, the snow-white perfection of her smooth skin looked genuine. This one looked like a certified trophy mistress.

Despite her plastic appearance, her calculated demeanor clashed with her looks: somehow she seemed too aggressive, assured and independent to be dependent on someone else's wealth. Her high ponytail bounced smoothly as it caressed its slender owner, yet her black cat suit was ravished with asymmetrical cutout shapes exposing her well-toned body. Her appearance was studied anarchy: haute couture for those who feigned abhorrence to haute couture.

The man in the suit considered what the plastic woman asked. The only way to find out what her game was, would have to be to fall into her predictable trap. "What do I think of it? I think it's a beautiful and loving tribute to those who are forced to face their mortality, but choose to do it with dignity and love."

The young woman frowned as she shook her head decisively and issued her verdict: "No, that is a rather tasteless sculpture, actually. It has no style, no voice, no spark. So much effort wasted! What is the point? Getting dirty and dried-out hands for what? For a static, never-changing lump that can never truly communicate with its audience. How unimaginative and pitiful."

The man grew upset with the reply, but tried to contain his disgust. "How could you say such a thing? What could possibly be wrong with this work of beauty?" he asked tersely as he studied the young woman's face.

She seemed annoyed at the question as she sighed. "If you must insist on me spelling out the logic behind my obvious conclusions, then I suppose it would be poor manners not to divulge them to you. Art must ambush its audience. It must mold and define. Art must talk to its audience..." The woman glanced coldly at the man as she studied his reaction. His anger had not abated.

After trying to suppress her smirk, she continued her lecture. "But it cannot merely repeat the same phrase over and over again as it stands still on the wall or on its pedestal. Communication is a two-way process. Language requires feedback and feedback keeps the cycle of exchange and enlightenment alive and dynamic. Art must overpower and then seduce its targets, before making them beg for more. How much more of this beige lump can you stand, before you are inclined to abandon it for another impotent and immobile diversion? Art must work to work. It cannot stand idly by and let lesser intellects define and interpret it. It must impose its powerful will on its audience, to break them, shatter their puerile delusions and comforts, and then show them what life is really all about!"

The young woman suddenly leaned against the offending statue, seemingly exhausted by her own lengthy sermon. It was a choreographed and old routine, the man was certain as he watched the B-list performance. There was a reason for her over-the-top oration; the man suspected the reason, but kept his theory to himself.

"All right," he finally answered coolly. "Why should an artist insult her audience with her work? Why would anyone support someone who has contempt for him?"

"Because it is the least he can do to atone for his ignorance! Because what the artist tells him is the truth! Because," the young woman nearly shouted in an angry, cracking voice as she gazed wild-eyed at the man, "art is life and life is art!"

All that bombast and cogitation for a clichéd zenith. The man shook his head and walked away. He had no time to engage in petty battles with lordly freaks, and even if he did, this was one woman with whom he did not wish to debate. She was too manipulative for comfort; her eyes revealed as much to him. Though he could not explain what sort of sickness resided in the base of her soul, the composition of it was clearly malevolent and calculating. He did not want to stay too long within her reach and began to make his way to the fringes of the crowded hub.

"Cool man! You had the honor of talking to the artist herself!" a disembodied, sarcastic and rippling male voice announced.

The man stopped and turned to his left to see who had made the remark. It was a young man, no older than twenty, smirking as they made eye contact.

"That arrogant and psychopathic twit is an artist? Who is she, anyway? I'd hate to think what she'd do to people in a dark alley."

"You never heard of Divinia Surrealist? Underground art queen of the universe? Where do you live?"

"Divinia Surrealist? Sounds tasteless enough to be an artist of note."

"Hey, she is the artist of note. Unfortunately."

"Then why are you here?"

"Because she's the artist of note," sighed the young man. "As crude as she is, she has her following, and it's a real devoted one. OK, maybe what she does isn't original, but you have to hand it to the girl, she knows how to sell her idea and how to shock a jaded crowd."

"Anything goes these days in these places, and it's been that way for a long, long time. I let myself drift away from this world, but even so, it shouldn't surprise me."

"So, why are you here?"

"Well, I didn't come for her, certainly. I just came in to see what the fuss was about. I hope she's not the only fuss around here."

"I'm sorry to burst your bubble, but there is no other reason why people would come here today."

The man in the suit groaned. "People are sheep. But you don't really thinks she believes that tripe she's shilling?"

"I think she believes in parts of it," the young man said slowly and pensively. "I think she revels in all the attention and the validation she gets from her fans and the media. I don't think she really believes art should violate people's brains, though. She just does that to get attention from the mainstream."

The older man shook his head as he straightened his coat. "I have a feeling that might be the only part she actually believes in. She seemed giddy to think that her work was disturbing to other people. Anyhow, I have to hurry; there is something here I want to get for my daughter, and still I still have a conference to attend. Good luck."

II

The swelling of suspense had just reached its breaking point: the artist herself was in full view of her audience, yet she still remained cool and seemingly unready to reveal her latest work. But her fans could not really accuse her of idle loafing, after all, her work could only be ready when the time was right and that was the one element out of her control. Divinia worked with unpredictable media and that was the price she had to pay for her choice of materials.

For the last hour Divinia seemed irritable, yet within seconds her mood changed. She peeked behind the curtain barrier and nodded seriously. It was show time.

Her audience seemed to sense that their patience was about to reap them satisfying dividends – the banal chatter ceased as the lady of the hour sauntered to the microphone.

"I grew up with enormous disadvantages," Divinia abruptly conceded to the crowd. She frowned. "I admit that my pedigree is highly lacking. My parents were the white-collar sort – computer programmers to be precise, which, as everyone knows, is the modern-day version of the blue-collar worker. They were pedestrian and plebeian, and entirely obsessed with lattes and impressing their pathetic friends with driving an expensive car. It was a horrifying and taxing childhood. My only refuge was my art and my belief that I was the love child of Salvador Dali and a schizophrenic Italian nun. If it weren't for my childhood Mignon delusions, I would have gone completely insane!"

The crowd cheered boisterously at their idol's confession.

Divinia looked with disgust at the crowd. "Well, if you are going to stand around like those lifeless statues, I don't see the point of wasting my valuable insights on you. It is because of people like you that I was forced to plunge to the depths of despair to find the Truth and thrust it all on you! Open the curtain! Open their minds!"

On cue, the burgundy-and-gold curtains slowly opened to reveal Divinia's latest offering: five black-leather- clad, ashen figures – three men and two women, shivering in front of the audience. All seemed disconnected, yet feral as they stood on the stage.

"Do you see those junkies up there, my children? Aren't they lovely?" Divinia cooed as she tenderly stroked her own arm. "Those feral, sunken eyes; those emaciated bodies that have endured track marks and hardened johns, and those uncontrollable tremors – all of those are singing their twisted little songs to you, my sweethearts. This is raw living. Feel it. Feel everything."

The crowd began to move toward the stage to study each unique piece as Divinia continued her lecture. "Notice, as each minute passes they become more edgy and desperate for another hit? They're missing their drugs, those poor things. See the neediness in the girl's eyes? She'd agree to do just about anything to get heroin flowing in her veins again. That's the dynamic wonders of my work. It's never the same piece of art twice. It's always screaming at you: the smells, the sites, the sound, and the touch. You are more than free to lick them if you want to get the full sensory experience. Just avoid the wounds and the scabs."

Some in crowd jumped on stage, taking their mistress' advice. Some began to poke or touch each piece; others merely stared at each figure, absorbing each breath and twitch they witnessed. The pieces stared back, some frightened, others edgy at the continued probing.

Divinia continued to speak, "I always loved Louis Wain's art,

108

well his later work, anyway. I have no use for his earlier scribbles."

"You mean the guy who drew cats, but then developed schizophrenia?" someone in the crowd asked.

"Ah, so you have heard of him." Divinia seemed disappointed that one of her fans had recognized the name. "Yes, I have an appreciation for the irreversible and tortuous fragmentation of his mind, but even so, I don't think he ventured deep enough into that fascinating little abyss. I always felt he tried to keep back just a bit. How sad. But there's something so wondrous about it. Watching people wither away. Seeing a luscious and beautiful young girl slowly transform herself into a putrid and ugly bag of bones – it's raw and it's rancid! It's squalor and it's splendor at the same time. Snorting that white powder and injecting that liquid into the flesh is more than the mere defiance of normalcy and free will: it is an irrefutable affirmation of the need for physical and spiritual slavery."

As the crowd continued to admire Divinia's latest artistic offerings, she took her mike and walked toward her work. The first human statue on stage was a defiant and bitter-looking woman; her once beautiful face ravaged by a lethal cocktail of drugs, hard living, and broken promises. She stood with her hands clenched, and her black leather bikini hanging oddly from her thin frame. Though she looked as she were about to speak, she remained brooding and silent.

"This one I call 'Auntie America.' You would not believe she's not even thirty years old yet, and already she's become an old and rotting pile of flesh who's willing to whore her decaying, decrepit goods for another cheap hit. But, I'm thinking it's not enough – perhaps I really should offer her up as part of my exhibit when I take this one to Amsterdam, providing she lives that long. What do you children think?"

The crowd cheered wildly with catcalls and lewd affirmations.

"Now this piece I call 'Fields' simply because he is so spaced-out. He kind of does nothing for ages and ages, and then he flips out in such a usual way. All right, Fields, show us your trick. Come on! Show it! You can do it, Fields. Show people your trick!"

After some terse verbal prodding from both Divinia and her beguiled followers, the emaciated young man with the long and dirty brown hair began to poke his arms and chest with a large and rusty safety pin. As his blood began to trickle down, the audience enthusiastically applauded, while their hostess smirked in amusement.

"See? You sometimes have to coax them into doing their thing, but it's worth the little effort for that kind of pay-off."

More unrestrained cheers from the crowd continued to flow as Divinia sauntered confidently to her next exhibit – a striking blonde man of eighteen who was clad in heavy, black leather boots. She stopped and paused for effect, then began to speak again. "I like this one. I call it 'Boots' because that's all this one wants to wear. You see, he's still not as far gone as Auntie America or Fields. He still has muscle and a fairly handsome visage. The problem with this one is that he's into crack and meth now, and that's going to ravage him in pretty short order. He still can pop a boner on demand, but he's not as good as he used to be. Pity."

By now, the piercing whooping and whistling made the room vibrate, yet, Divinia only smiled serenely as she walked over to a short, stout, and feral man who looked much older than his thirty years. The ruddy man was trembling as she playfully rubbed his bad, sweating head.

"This is one is called 'Atomic Bob' and it's almost my favorite. He'll drop any day now, which is a shame. He just goes off into his own psychotic little dimension where he's a warrior who has to save his people from carcinogenic pineapple ninja aliens. Watch him..." Divinia began to clap her hands in front of the man's face and yelled, "The aliens! The aliens!"

On cue, Atomic Bob's face contorted and reddened and he began to scream, and flail his flabby arms. He {began} started to run around in place, while his continued shouts about cancerous pineapple alien assassins amused his onlookers. After a minute of frenzied cursing and running, Atomic Bob jumped off the stage and into the audience, desperately trying to part the crowd and protect himself from the alien invasion. His mistress merely snapped her fingers and pointed to him before two security guards grabbed the paranoid man by his dog collar and hauled him back to his place on the stage. As one guard held him, the other took a black leash, attached it to the man's collar, then attached the other end to a heavy metal pole. Then, both men quickly returned to their original places.

After waiting for her audience to settle down, Divinia strolled over to her final piece – a waifish young woman, who sat slouched over on a black leather chair. "That's drama. Now, I call this one 'Mumbles,' and it's my personal favorite. Go ahead, anybody, ask her a question – anything at all."

An aggressively loud and husky male voice bawdily asked the frail, drained figure on stage if she liked to partake in coarse sexual escapades. The young woman looked pensively at her feet, then began to scrunch her nose and bite her lips in seemingly deep thought. The audience's cheering began to turn to stifled laughter and they anxiously waited for the animated woman to reply.

After a few moments, the face of the fragile woman in a leather corset and fishnet stockings lit up, she nodded giddily and replied enthusiastically, "Ah, waffa du dings du manny manny pwepples!"

The crowd cheered maniacally until Divinia raised her well-toned arm and waved her hand with an authoritative air. The base screams and hollers abruptly ceased.

"Mumbles represents intellectual confusion and communicative static in a modern age," Divinia explained to her fans. "Poor communication skills are always unfortunate, but at least Mumbles here, does it with much enthusiasm. Love her, men, because she's so eager to please you all … as they all are. They're all here for you, for your own personal enjoyment. Look, listen, and feel them. Become one with them. Reject them, abhor them, love them, pity them, but also watch them! Watch them waste away before your very eyes. See them now, because who knows if you'll ever see them on this stage again. Addicts can be such unpredictable media."

III

"...A disgusting, vile, carnivalesque freak show that is thinly disguised as 'cutting-edge 'art,' that's what you peddle."

"Spare me the faux indignation."

"You've become a vulture and a fraud!"

"Slander like that will make you a poorer man, I assure you."

"You're promoting the gutter and justifying its existence. How can you live with yourself?"

"Promoting the gutter? Justifying its existence? Hardly. I am just doing my small part to beautify it. And it's made me very, very rich, too."

"Your brazen smugness is going to cost you dearly one day. You're too reckless and crass."

"Crass? Yes, perhaps I have been guilty of using a small splash of it in my work, but then again, I use so many other colors: grimness, grit, horror, truth, style, panache, and a touch of crass. Those are the colors of my rainbow."

"Don't play those pretentious word games with me! I'm not one of your drooling fan boys anymore and I'm not a fawning journalist hungry for a colorful sound bite. There are a lot of powerful people who don't like what you're doing – and they have a vested interest in stopping your little juggernaut..."

"...I am not in the least concerned about their petty jealousies..."

"Let me finish. They don't like you, they resent what you've done to their galleries, they hate the fact you're stealing the limelight from some of their children in the business, and they especially don't like the fact that you're using that Lassiter girl in your shows."

"My exhibit absolutely depends on having Auntie America in it…"

"…She also used to be a call girl for some pretty rich and powerful men. That girl knows too many secrets as it is. Those suits are all terrified that for publicity, you're going to have her spill her guts during one of your upcoming shows. That's what everyone's been buzzing about and you know it. They know you're ruthless and shameless – and that you're not above using any cheap or dangerous stunt to get what you want."

"It's not up to me if she decides to use my exhibit as a confessional…"

"It doesn't matter. You're flirting with danger. You already have gotten searched by police for drugs…"

"I don't carry them and I don't have them in my home, car, or studio…"

"If they can't nail you for drugs, they'll do something worse. Make no mistake: they are going to get you one day, Molly. They are going to make an example out of you. You're too clever and cheeky for your own good."

"I take precautions."

"You also take too many risks."

"I know who and what I'm up against, but that won't stop me.

They rejected me; they put every obstacle in my way. They'll pay for that one way or another. Auntie will break her silence very soon. I've been working on her. But she still thinks some of her old clients are going to come to her rescue, if you can believe it. That's why she agreed to be part of my show – for the publicity. The reality of her abandonment is starting to sink in, though, even through that drug-fueled deluded mess she calls a brain. But I can't force it; all I can do is offer the right incentive and wait."

"Molly, I hate what you've become. I remember when you were that cute little sassy girl who sculpted elaborate statues of children playing with kittens. Every guy in art school was so in love with you, me included. You are an incredibly talented artist with a pretty face, but you've changed for the worse. This is a hard profession with nothing but rejection and scathing criticism. You can't let it get to you. The road's a hard go for everybody, not just you! You're better than this and you know it."

"Better doesn't sell and talent doesn't open the door of salvation when you're alone in the wilderness. Everything I valued and cherished became chains that kept me back. They won't let you in if you're truly good because it makes them look bad, and they can't have that. But a stunt here and a scam there gets them distracted enough to open that door just enough for you to sneak in. But you have to know how to play their game better than they do. That Lassiter girl didn't start out as a junkie, you know. None of them did. All those freaks started out as ambitious and talented, and all got eaten alive. They've all got secrets, by the way, not just Auntie. When she finally breaks, they all will, and when the tabloids get a load of it, all those smug gatekeepers will look just as trashy as the rest of us. It's going to be quite the show."

"They won't let that happen."

"How will they stop me?"

"They have the resources and the will. Don't risk it."

"It's too late to stop it now – and I won't back down after all the work and risks I've put into it. I'll see you tonight after the show, Wes. Oh, come on, don't look so gloomy. Everything will work out, and then you can focus your energies on rehabilitating hopeless old me, if that's what turns you on. Bye, you."

IV

The mildly disappointed crowd had long ago showed themselves
out of the gallery, leaving behind five leather-clad drug addicts
huddling and whispering together on stage, while their employer
and the night's star attraction was pacing pensively by the dais.
Divinia was not pleased with either the end result or with herself:
there was an element she didn't factor into her equation and her
miscalculation had delayed her victory.

Nothing presented itself as extraordinary, yet nothing was going
according to plan. Tonight was supposed to be big; it was supposed to be Divinia's *tour de force*, and yet everything was going
horribly, horribly wrong. First, her living statues were over three
hours late in arriving at the museum. While drug addicts weren't
known to be reliable, this tardiness was particularly galling. All
five had been late this time, and when they all finally arrived,
they were both surly and unresponsive. Atomic Bob wouldn't
scream or throw his dazzling tantrum. Mumbles wouldn't speak.
Fields seemed more alert than usual and wouldn't prick himself
with his rusty pin, and Boots made no attempt to arouse himself
for the audience. But the worst offender and biggest disappointment was Auntie America.

The Lassiter girl seemed ready to spill her secrets the night before, yet tonight she remained as angry and tightlipped as ever.
She refused to even glance in Divinia's direction, which meant
Divinia's plan faced its worst setback yet. This was not good. If
Auntie decided to keep her salacious and toxic knowledge to
herself, then there was no point continuing with this farce of an
haute underground circus. An elaborate setup without even a
decent payoff was out of the question: Divinia would have to
think of a new way to exact her revenge.

She glanced up and looked at mass of black leather and pale skin
hunkering down and murmuring in conspiratorial tones. Some

game was afoot among them. Mutiny? A clumsy plan to demand a bigger piece of the pie? No matter, unless Auntie told all at tomorrow night's showing, their gig would be officially terminated.

"What are you pathetic, good-for-nothing creatures whispering about?" Divinia yelled as she slapped the wooden dais with her hand, "You're lateness and laziness nearly ruined the exhibit. Everything depends on your behavior – and tonight was an absolute disgrace! Don't expect to get paid unless you deliver the goods."

"Can it, sister," Boots snapped angrily, "We don't need you anymore."

"Unless you've decided to swear off crack – which I seriously doubt – you all desperately need me *and* your next hit right about now. And, Lassiter, what was with you clamming up tonight of all nights? You damn well know I didn't hire you for your pretty face – you either give me what we agreed upon tomorrow, or this show is officially over. I'm not paying you people to loaf around the stage – I expect results!"

"We've had just about enough of you," spat Auntie America, approaching Divinia with a clenched fist. "You're no better than those rich johns who promised me heaven and then drove me straight to hell. Enough is enough."

"Spare me your sob stories! You've no one but yourself to blame for your mess. I've given you countless chances to get your revenge on those well-heeled louts, but you conveniently refused to take them. I'm beginning to think you like to be human sewage!"

"Hey, girly," Atomic Bob suddenly bellowed as he turned toward Divinia, "The woman said she had enough of you. And you know something? We all have!"

"It's time to teach her a lesson," Fields said excitedly.

"Let's make a painting from her blood," Boots yelled.

Without giving her a second to react on the direness of her situation, Bob leaped across the dais, grabbed Divinia by the arm and threw her across the stage. As the stunned woman tried to gather her wits, Mumbles ran toward her and tried to grab her target's long blonde hair, but the flaxen tresses turned out to be nothing more than a wig made from human hair. As Mumbles stood holding the disembodied wig, Divinia quickly jumped off the makeshift stage and began to run toward the exit. Behind her were her one-time exhibits, furiously chasing her.

None of this made any sense, she thought as she searched for safety. Where were the guards? There was always someone at the museum when they left for the night: why was it so empty? Why did her subjects suddenly turn against her? Why were they so bloodthirsty without warning or provocation?

The front door was within reach, yet, Divinia almost instinctually knew, that her ticket to freedom would be locked. Whatever plot transpired tonight, it was diabolical; this was a premeditated attack; she was absolutely sure of it. Yet, the five addicts chasing her were hardly coherent or shrewd enough to plan this by themselves, or be able to persuade security to leave her alone with them. But who was responsible for this conspiracy? What was the motive? There was no time to for her to ponder who or what instigated this revolt against her. Her creations were quickly surrounding her and seemed determined to inflict mortal damage upon her lithe body.

V

"Working late tonight?" the young man in the black suit asked his employer, a gray-haired gentleman of fifty who sat behind his large, glass desk, working on his client's cases.

The older man looked up and shook his head. "No, I've been invited to see a new exhibit by some up-and-coming artist this evening. Not exactly something I'd normally bother myself with, but Cassie insisted that I come to see his work. She's the artsy one in the family, and a big supporter of the museum. I never had an interest in that sort of thing."

"So who's the artist?"

"Don't know anything about it except what my wife's told me. It's supposed to be some edgy and daring new sculptor. At least, I hope this isn't another manipulator like Divinia Surrealist. One of her was all we could take," the older man snapped angrily.

The young was taken aback by both the mention of Divinia's name and his employer's impassioned reaction. "I haven't heard that name in at least a couple of years, not since she disappeared after one of her shows. No one knows what happened to her. Some people say she killed herself after one of her shows flopped here."

"Yes," mumbled the gray-haired man as he furiously scribbled nothing in particular on his memo pad, "there are rumors she finally cracked and ended it all with a leap into the river. It's a rumor, of course, but what else can explain her disappearance? She was associating with, and abusing those psychotic junkies, and was probably as mentally stable as they were. Who knows? Perhaps the other rumors are true: that her druggies turned on her, tortured her, then they even pushed her in the river them-selves."

"Probably," the young man said meekly, "but I find it a little odd that all those junkies were found frozen to death in an alley, but her body was nowhere to be found."

"I am certain there are many people who were just happy all that decrepit human trash was finally taken away. Whatever transpired that night, those repugnant beasts all took their miserable little secrets into their unmarked graves. If Divinia were still alive, there is no way in hell that woman would keep silent for this long. She's burning in hell as we speak."

"I remember reading about that case in some magazine. It said that all the junkies overdosed on pure heroin. I wonder where they got it."

"They most likely killed her for the drugs she was doling out to them. Enough about that," the older man replied curtly. "Let's get back to work."

VI

The collective anticipation at the gallery that evening was restrained, but tastefully aroused. The affair was by invitation-only, and the guests spent some time with the standard solicitous chit chat. The seasoned, well-heeled invitees strolled around the museum, taking in the various sites: from the Mennonite quilts, black-and-white photographs of impoverished children, to the cordoned off center room that teased its audience with a thick red-and-gold curtain hiding the evening's delights.

Waiting impatiently by the velvet ropes was a gray-haired man in an impeccably tailored suit and his lanky, graceful wife. The man looked around the room nervously, unmoved by the quilts or the photographs. His pacing was upstaged only by his repeated glances at his watch.

"Would you please clam down?" his wife finally pleaded as she touched his arm, "You were less edgy when we sent Dylan off to Fairmont College!"

"I have better things to do than loaf around here, waiting for some starving artist to make an appearance. Why hasn't he come out yet and what's with all this secrecy? Who is this person, anyway? You never did get around to telling me."

"I don't know; the invitations didn't say who it was."

"Cassie, do you mean to tell me that you have no idea who the artist is?"

"That's part of the charm, Jon! It's supposed to be a surprise."

"Well, I don't like surprises. It reminds me too much of that Divinia character."

"Don't be paranoid. You know the museum would know better than to associate themselves with someone who's trying to imitate someone who brought shame to our arts community."

"I never heard of such a thing. How are they supposed to promote the exhibit, if they don't reveal who the artist in question is? How would patrons know if they'd want to go see it when they don't know what kind of work they'll be showing?"

"It's supposed to be a mystery theme," one bystander chimed in at hearing the terse exchange. "The invitation said that this artist uses puzzles and riddles as his theme; so, what better way to drum up some publicity than by keeping his identity a secret? It's sort of like a mystery dinner theater, except instead of dinner, it's art. Kind of quaint, actually."

"Stunts! I don't trust artists who have to rely on stunts," the older man fumed and he shook his head.

"Jon, I don't understand your attitude. Relax and enjoy the evening!"

"I don't want to indulge another Divinia-wannabe."

"What's your obsession with her? You've never even been to one of her exhibits, and yet you've done nothing but rant about her, even years after her disappearance! I really wonder about you…"

"Ladies and Gentlemen," a nervous male voice interrupted, "the show is about to begin."

"And what a show it will be. A million puzzles will be solved tonight and a million more riddles will be posed," a terse and haughty female voice boomed across the room. The eerie voice pierced the jovial mood, and in unison, the crowd turned around to see who the mystery artist was.

It *was* Divinia.

The crowd moaned in agony.

Despite all the rumors of her mistreatment at the hands of her exhibits, Divinia looked as plastic and assured as ever. Not a scar marred her face nor did she seem to have any sort of physical trauma impeding her gait or her movements. She was as toned and calm as ever, though her trademark blonde hair was replaced with short black hair. She looked both smug and intense; calm and enraged. Her presence and her demeanor seemed to frighten her guests.

"Surprised? Shocked? Disappointed? The evening's only just begun; get a hold of yourselves, you have seen nothing yet."

"We thought you were dead," spluttered one dazed guest.

"You've been misinformed."

"What happened? Those junkies…," began one woman before she was cut off.

"…were supposed to kill me? Is that what you were going to say? Yes, they did make something of an attempt on my life, but fortunately, they were too far gone in their addiction and insanity, to be able to go against someone who has a black belt in several forms of martial arts, including Wing Chun. Don't you know Wing Chun? It's a nice one to know when you're cornered in tight spaces. An artist must be skilled in her craft, and when you are dealing with uninhibited brutes, self-defense is as useful a tool as a paint brush. Suffice it to say they didn't have a prayer, and I saved myself. I was also fortunate enough that one of my acquaintances came here that evening to see me. It is thanks to him I managed to get to safety and keep hidden these past two years."

"What are you up to now? Are we supposed to be impressed by these games?" the man in the gray suit asked angrily.

"Games?" Divinia said slowly as if to contain her anger. "I play no games; I play for keeps. It was a very hard going for me that evening, but I wasn't going to lose, no matter what. That night, it meant everything to me to live another day. It meant absolutely everything. Money and fame used to mean everything until that night, but then…" She paused, took a long deliberate breath, and continued.

"Nothing means anything when you have money. It's the ugly little secret that everyone wants to deny. You can buy fame. You can hire the smartest minds to write your college papers for you. Awards are obtainable by having the right connections and hiring the right mouthpieces to shill your pseudo-achievements for you. Daddies with money can get you a movie, book, or TV deal. Money can even keep you out of jail when you're guilty and make a mockery out of the system of justice. So, what does it all mean anyway? When money can get that something for you, it suddenly becomes worthless. Any shopaholic will tell you that buying is the rush, but owning is the crash.

"But," Divinia purred as she walked purposefully toward the center of her concealed exhibit, "vitriol and cruelty are priceless. All that cash can't repair what a single, cutting remark can destroy – the very essence of your fragile soul. No amount of shuttling between your shrink and your pharmacist will save you. Buy your precious little presidency … if I drive your precious little prince or princess down that one-way path of self-loathing destruction, you become nothing! It's the ultimate exercise in futility. Firing your powerful sperm toward a dead-end street!

"Money. Power. Fame. Yes, in a pinch they are still nice little trinkets to have, but without unrestrained and unfiltered malice, what are they really worth?"

"Save your sermons for your barbaric disciples," sneered one of the patrons as he wagged his finger at his object of scorn.

"Oh, that wasn't a sermon," Divinia said thoughtfully. She straightened her short black hair with her hand. "That was the preface to my newest exhibit. It's the biggest and best one yet. I confess that the last batch of pieces turned out to be...*somewhat defective*, but that was because a few cowardly beings with money and influence made it their business to sabotage my work. Well, their plan backfired; I survived, and I'm back. Wait until you see this *tour de force*..."

"What now? You found a new set of street trash to flaunt?"

"Oh, no," replied a chillingly serene Divinia. "The problem with the last one was embarrassingly obvious: those pieces were already hardened addicts when I plucked them from obscurity. This time, I decided to start with a fresh, clean canvas and mold it precisely the way I wanted..."

The uneasiness of the crowd began to show at once. Some immediately grasped Divinia's cryptic hints, while others began to fidget and stared nervously, not completely certain what horrible surprise was being kept behind the curtain. The only *calm* figure in the room relished her audience's near panic.

"I admit it took a while to do it. Everything had to be so hush-hush about it at first. Tip off the wrong people and the plan would blow up in my face. I couldn't arouse suspicions; so everything had to be about winning confidences, and doing everything one little bit at a time. Fortunately, parental neglect and surprisingly lax screening processes at boarding schools made my paranoia virtually unnecessary. Using my birth name and toning down my appearance to get a position as an art teacher also helped…"

"If you did what I think you've done," started one red-faced woman, but Divinia raised her hand as if to shoo her away.

"Of course I did," she quipped giddily as she pulled the rope to lift the curtain shrouding her work. "As for smuggling my work in here, a little blackmail goes a long way when confronting certain guilty parties who took an active part in the plot to kill me. But enough of that. Meet the new collection. I call this series *Wain in Vain!*"

As the curtain rose, the nervous spectators looked toward the stage: there were ten teenagers on it – the oldest could be no more than seventeen. Their dazed, disconnected appearances contrasted with their boarding school uniforms. None of the teens seemed coherent; one was clearly drooling; another was rolling his eyes as he swayed back and forth. One girl was muttering gibberish to herself. Behind each of the ten was a collage of paintings: the top pictures were all well-drawn, yet every subsequent painting below the previous became increasingly fragmented and disturbing.

"That's Dylan! That's our child up there!" Cassie screamed as she stared at her son on stage.

"You're observant," Divinia replied dryly.

She perkily popped on stage and began to speak anew. "You see, the rich can be so careless with certain possessions. They're too busy with their careers, their libidos, their bragging rights, and their meaningless, air-headed rivalries and vendettas to notice when their children have been away from home too long. But, you know what they say – one man's trash is another man's treasure!

"See how each living sculpture is surrounded by its own works of art? Each painting serves as a milestone as they progressed into that little abyss called insanity. You can see their tender little brains disintegrating and imploding with each painting they cre- ated. I encouraged them to surpass Louis Wain – and they did! Their young minds and souls are already dead now; it's the drugs animating the bodies. When art melds with science and immorality, anything is possible. It is nothing short of a miracle: they had no idea how potent and damaging the drugs I gave them tonight really were. It was truly, truly a beautiful thing to see," Divinia cooed, {as she held} her hands together as if she were about to pray.

"Did you think you can…," one man started lunging toward Divinia, who effortlessly leaped out of harm's way.

"What? Get away with this? I already did."

"I'll see you in hell for what you've done!"

"That's where you'll be seeing a lot of people, including them," cooed Divinia as she winked at her stunned, fuming prey, jerked her head toward her exhibit, and smirked.

The Footnote

I

If our deaths were any indication of the lives we led to the very last second, then Madeline was the most wretched being on earth. Period.

If our lives were a foreshadowing of our deaths; then Madeline would have gone peacefully in her sleep. Period.

Our lives and our deaths are just that: separate entities that collide for only one brief moment in time, merely to diverge and never cross paths again. Life and death are polar opposites; cacophony, dichotomy, the epitome of the Manichean universe. Nothing else in our world is that black-and-white, except black and white.

Madeline was a kind, gentle soul who was too naive for her own good. How shall I say: she had a heart of gold, which she wore upon her sleeve; not the type who sang her own praises while beating her own drum. She was a nice little girl who cared and worried, and helped whenever she could. She believed in causes and crusades, but did so silently and never told anyone what she was doing nor what they should be doing. She was not a prig, but a guardian angel. It was such a shame a girl like Madeline died the way she did. She should have been a legend, a role model, a good example for children everywhere...

But good, captivating stories do not use diligent waifs like Madeline as their centerpiece. Madeline, despite her perfection, can only be used as a footnote – a catalyst at the most – but no more. No, Madeline was a victim that did not triumph; therefore I am left no choice but to digress. This story isn't about Madeline – but about Stuart.

Stuart – the man ultimately responsible for poor Maddie's demise – was the nice blend of Darwin, Bismarck, and Machiavelli; therefore he had no qualms of bringing Maddie's existence to an abrupt end. What needed to be done was done. Things had to go smoothly in order to benefit the collectivity; hence the sacrifice of one person was better than the sacrifice of the majority. Perhaps Stuart was, in the most twisted sense of the concept, Jeremy Benthem's bastard son. If there was one redeeming quality about Stuart, it was that he did not let anyone spoil the fun for everyone else. But, most important: Stuart triumphed; so it is with him we must begin our tale.

II

Dirtied floors, drab walls, old desks, outdated room dividers, wobbly chairs, dim lights, droning noises, and stale air: to the naïve and industrious, it meant yet another day of soul-numbing drudgery. To Stuart, it meant a decent cover and even more decent returns. The workplace could deaden the sharpest of minds – so long as they foolishly chose to come in every morning and then chose to work at the job they were hired to do. Stuart, on the other hand, would not agree to such ludicrous terms that were both demoralizing and grossly unprofitable.

But he was not entirely unsympathetic to the needs of his employers, after all, they did provide him with the opportunity to obtain his wealth and he had to return the favor. At this particular place of employment, no one cared what the worker ants were doing so long as if they seemed to *work*. Faking busy was easier than actually being busy. Walking, while looking down at a full folder, was easy enough to do, as was staring at a computer screen or scribbling on a pad during a meeting. As long as Grundman saw the requisite motions, he made no other demands. Slacker bosses were easy to please, and Stuart gladly obliged.

The difficult part was the *real* work, and there Stuart had to take more precautions. At first, the upside was that the firm made money – enough money, anyway – not to notice when a couple of hundred here or there never made it to the company's coffers; however, one had to be careful about not taking too much, or too often – knowing *when* and *how much* was not a simple code to break. Sometimes there would be a sluggish quarter or another unforeseeable event and one had to hold back until the timing was right again, but even then, restraint and vigilance was needed. Even more difficult was to ensure that those missing funds would never be recorded in any of the company's books or files. That sort of paper trail could prove to be a fatal mistake.

However, as time went on Stuart quickly learned that certain *other* paper trails were in fact desirable, and more important: more *profitable*. A shell company here and a bogus supplier there would bring in thousands of dollars instead of some paltry hundreds. The firm had a strong desire to contract out certain services to third-party companies, even if those services weren't exactly needed. However, "contracting out" sounded more fiscally prudent than "in-house," so whenever tasks that were formerly "in- house" could now be "contracted out," the firm was happy. If Stuart and his cohorts could create the illusion of a "third party" to provide these services, then they could be happy, while Grundman could impress his superiors with his department's efficiency and be left alone. Stuart made certain that everyone could be happy: the overlords would have enough profits to buy their yachts and entertain their mistresses; Grundman would be free to keep a sleepy eye on his underlings while playing office golf, and Stuart and his cohorts would be free to seem busy, while secretly increasing their disposable income and help improve the economy. It was a win-win-win situation and Stuart was the able captain of this buoyant ship.

But, keeping the crew happy was a difficult and dangerous undertaking that required constant watching and finesse. Stuart needed to coax and cajole his conspirators to act busy while keeping tabs on Grundman and the overlords, and his coworkers were more than happy to help out so that they could reach the same level of contentment. But even then, Stuart had to keep certain confidences to himself and while Sally and Phil were aware of certain Truths, they did not know how profitable his real work was. Had they known, they could easily demand a bigger piece of his happiness, or choose to blackmail him into giving them nearly the entire bliss. Trust had to be used sparingly.

Not that Stuart wanted to trust either of his co-workers at all this morning. They both were behaving like two shallow juveniles. Sally seemed to repeatedly obsess over her large nose and small breasts, instead of appearing to be working diligently and quietly at her work station. The topic of her physical defects came up often, but today, she seemed to talk of nothing else. Grundman would not be happy, and when Grundman was unhappy, he became anxious and uncontrollable, making Stuart unhappy. Misery was an unprofitable frame of mind.

Then there was Phil.

The old, greasy, corpulent windbag was at it again that morning.

"I'm sick," he whined and winced in pain at his overflowing desk.

"Yeah?" Stuart asked as he began to read his email. "How are you sick?"

"I'm bored."

"That ain't bein' sick!"

"It is too. I've got nothin' and nothin' to do. I'm just sittin' around waiting to retire."

"You got plenty to do," whispered Stuart as he gave his cohort a sharp, knowing glare. "You gotta look busy. Everything depends on you and Sally doing that. So start acting busy and you won't be sick."

"I know, I know," Phil conceded in an undertone, "it's just that I'm sick of being forced to pretend to do something!"

"Shhh!"

"I know."

"Then shut up, will you?"

"I know."

"My boobs just totally suck," interrupted Sally, looking down inside her satin, mauve-colored blouse. "I mean, look at that! Nibs! I just got nibs. What kind of guy wants to feel up nibs?"

"Are we supposed to feel sorry for you, Sally?" snapped Stuart. He shot an authoritative glance at his newest annoyance.

"Yeah! Do you want to feel these up?" Sally asked, pointing at her modest chest.

"No."

"See? I bet you would cop a feel if they were bigger than nibs."

"Would you keep it down, Sally? Don't let Grundman hear you."

"I don't care if he hears! He won't want to feel these up, any-way. How am I supposed to land myself a rich husband with my big nose and little boobs? I didn't get this job to *work!*"

"Keep it down or you won't be landing a sugar daddy in jail," Stuart hissed.

Sally merely rolled her eyes as she readjusted her blouse just as Grundman brusquely opened the door. With Grundman, every-thing was abrupt; no preamble, no preface. Stuart was used to Grundman's tornadoesque manners; he simply suppressed his annoyance and slowly turned around to face the stout, balding, middle-aged man with a slight, irritating slouch.

What was this? A young attractive woman was walking one step behind Grundman! She was too spry and alert to be a new secretary. She was just slightly too old and too well-dressed to be a lowly intern – she was still young enough to be eager, and just old enough to be the owner of a graduate degree. This was not good news. A smart, new, ambitious keener could make a lot of formerly happy employees very unhappy.

"Everyone, I would like you to meet our newest employee Madeline," Mr. Grundman began with his usual lack of grace or forewarning. Phil and Sally looked up. Phil obviously liked the shape of the new piece of fresh meat; Sally was insanely jealous and made no attempt to hide her disdain. Both were looking directly at the young woman's lush chest. Stuart held his breath and studied first Grundman, then Madeline.

Madeline reeked of goodness and trouble.

"It's nice to meet you all," the young woman said as she extended her manicured hand toward Stuart.

This was not good, Stuart thought as he extended his wiry hand to his newest obstacle, and object of misery. The feel of Madeline's small, soft hand and its firm, friendly grip simply underscored her undying adherence to rules and to protocol. This one sincerely believed in ethics, morals, and diligence. Bitch.

"This is Stuart," Grundman said to his newest charge, "and this is Sally and this is Phil."

"It's nice to meet you, Stuart," the young woman said deliberately as she studied him carefully. "You can call me, Maddie, by the way. I'm really looking forward to work with you."

Stuart wondered why.

Maddie was studying him carefully.

She was not as green as she looked. Her smile was too serene and knowing. Her eyes were too sharp.

If that was the case, then was Grundman really as naïve as he looked? Why did he hire Maddie without mentioning a word of it to anyone? Grundman was not a man to keep secrets. This was not normal protocol.

Maddie's sudden appearance was definitely not going to make anyone happy, least of all Stuart.

III

Wednesday afternoons usually had a certain sweetness to them – once you get past them, you know more than half the working week is already under your belt, thought Stuart as he smoked his last cigarette in the back alley during his lunch break. Three days down, two more to go before the weekend. There was light at the end of the tunnel. There were just two more days of Madeline before the weekend.

Madeline was now Mr. Grundman's favorite employee. She came in before everyone else and left work after everyone else did. She was by far the most productive worker in the office. Stuart sneered in disgust as he recalled seeing Maddie working quietly at her desk during lunch. She was always putting more effort than cunning into her work.

Stuart dropped his smoke and crushed it with his shoe before he walked back inside the building and to his desk. With Madeline at the office, his extracurricular activities had to be executed with extreme caution and unprecedented sleight of hand. His nemesis knew where every paper clip was located; she also had an impeccable understanding of corporate structures, finances, and cash flow. She was quick with numbers; she could not only crunch them; she could beat the secrets right out of them.

Life wasn't always so complicated. Maddie had started a mere eight months ago and she had already received one raise and two promotions. She hadn't even exchanged a single sexual favor for them. Poor Sally had to date Mr. Grundman for two years before she saw a few pennies added to her paycheck.

Madeline made everyone unhappy. She was seriously threatening Stuart's bottom line. This was not acceptable, but he could not strike at her. He did not know how much she knew or what she may have suspected, but her repeated darting glances between him and her computer screen did not bode well for his bliss. Her quick, closed-lipped smiles did nothing to ease his fears.

Even Sally and Phil had begun to have their own set of neuroses over Madeline: Sally was no longer merely jealous of her co-worker's assets and button nose; she now seriously feared Grundman would discard her for the prettier female. Phil, who had once enjoyed ogling the comely new recruit, had grown to resent the young woman's rapid rise and feared she would soon have the power to fire him, or even worse, make some demands that he work. Both had finally understood that there were worse things Madeline could do to all of them if she stumbled upon their secret fountain of joy.

Stuart slowly walked to his cubicle as he continued to ponder what to do with Madeline.

A pleasant, if somewhat serious voice broke his thoughts. "Stuart, can I talk to you for a moment?" It was Madeline.

"Make it quick. I have a lot of work to do."

"I've been looking over some of our expenses this morning…"

"And?" Stuart replied nonchalantly as he held his breath.

"Well, there's something a bit off."

"I'm not the bean counter around here…"

"I know, but I thought I should tell you, because I was going over this with…"

A vexed voice interrupted Madeline and commanded, "Stuart!

Come into my office. I need to have a talk with you."

It was Grundman.

IV

"We have a problem with you, Stuart."

Grundman dropped the lower half of his face for effect. In psychological retaliation, Stuart started at his employer with his apathetic eyes. Mr. Grundman lobbed the brush-off by straightening his back and leaning forward. Stuart folded his arms and crossed his legs. Grundman clenched his fists and glared at his employee. Stuart remained silent. I'm not blinking or breaking, he thought, you are not going to control my movements.

One full minute passed. Silence.

And another. Nothing.

A third one would have gone by as well, but Grundman realized the only way to break the impasse was to give in. He did not want to waste his afternoon with Stuart.

 "Madeline says there's something strange about our Allworth deal because of you."

Stuart shook his head calmly. "What does she think is wrong with it?" Allworth was one of his shell companies and to make matters worse, it was by far the most lucrative.

"She says there is something fishy about their invoicing."

Stuart sighed and replied calmly, "Madeline is wrong. I wished she'd get her facts right, before bothering you with her theories of why she thinks a company's new, more efficient billing system is suspect. She's a sharp girl, that Maddie, but in this case, she's off by a mile. What makes her think there is something wrong with it? And why would she think it had anything to do with me? I am not responsible for another company's invoices."

Grundman did not expect the torrent of calm words from his most wound up employee. Stuart usually started to rant and rave. But then Stuart was usually in the wrong. Grundman pondered the possibilities. Madeline was always right and Stuart always wrong. But now, Stuart was not behaving wrongly. He was calm and confident. If he were bluffing, why would he ask for the evidence against him in a calm and rational manner, and why give his accuser any credit? He must be sure of himself, thought Grundman as he pressed and rolled his thin, deflated lips. He's either innocent or he covered his tracks well, but either way, it was only fair to return the favor. Besides, it would be too much work if he didn't.

Grundman filled his lungs with the room's flat air, shook his head and smiled. "Well, Stuart, you've convinced me. I'm sorry to have bothered you like this. I don't know what Maddie was thinking, but she's usually right about those things. I'll have a talk with her later. You can go back to your desk."

Stuart closed the door behind him. He went to the bathroom and locked the door. Then he began to think.

Maddie was becoming a big problem. Sooner or later, someone in the office was going to get fired or arrested on the account of that woman and he wasn't entirely convinced that Grundman wouldn't take a harder look at the Allworth contract, or worse, ask Maddie to look into it more closely. It would spoil the entire operation. It would never be the same again. Sure, Grundman was a screecher, but he could be kept in line. But Maddie was another story.

Maddie was a hard worker and a good employee who was loyal to her job. She wasn't going to go away by force or by choice.

Maddie couldn't be bribed into silence.

She couldn't be blackmailed.

She couldn't be bullied.

She couldn't be frightened.

She couldn't be manipulated.

Money, sex, compliments or threats couldn't keep her quiet.

There was only one way to keep Maddie quiet for as long as he needed.

V

It took a lot of quick, deliberate planning, but Stuart, Phil, and Sally had finally found a simple solution to their problem. For all her sharp thinking, Maddie had made a fortuitous miscalculation: she merely suspected that Stuart alone had some involvement with the suspect Allworth contract. She did not suspect that either Phil or Sally had any connection to the scheme.

This gave Stuart the leverage he so desperately needed. He had managed to alter and purge some of the pertinent Allworth documents, though even this was no guarantee that his adventures in financial ecstasy would not be quickly discovered. More important, he had managed to create a bogus document implicating his guilt. This he gave to Sally. This was the bait to lure his prey.

And good old Sally actually managed to look away from her chest long enough to pull through. She approached Madeline, on the pretense of finding some incriminating documents against Stuart – but she feared so much for her safety, she wanted to speak to Madeline alone, at another location. And, yes, because of the nature of the evidence, she did not want anyone else to know about her discovery. A sympathetic and gullible Madeline agreed to a fearful Sally's conditions. That Sally -- what a doll she was.

Phil also pulled through for the home team, when he agreed to provide the pivotal alibi that both Stuart and Sally would need. The benefits of teamwork were invaluable.

Most wonderfully, Madeline stuck to the script like a pro: she came alone at the designated time; she willingly went inside the abandoned building that was designated a private enough meeting spot; and she came in calling for Sally, still unaware of what was about to happen.

It was time to act.

Stuart grabbed Madeline by her long blonde hair and rapidly coiled it around his fist for a better grip. She began to scream. To this point, Madeline had never been in any trouble in her life. Stuart had full control and she fully comprehended the graveness of her situation. Even in the worst circumstance, she was incapable of lying to herself.

Stuart knew there were only two options. The first was that he would kill Maddie quickly, without any fuss. No bells or whistles: just a nice, easy killing. All it would take would be one efficient conk on the head or a letter opener into the heart. That would be simple. Maddie wouldn't suffer, and he wouldn't have to worry as much about someone walking in on his work. The main reason she had to die was to preserve the sanctity of his and his coworker's existence. Get the job done quickly was a good, smart choice: it was the clean and efficient way to do business.

It was the Maddie-way to do business.

But he hated Maddie's way of doing business.

He opted for the second option.

VI

It was five years before anyone found what was left Madeline's body. Even hard-bitten policemen considered the find "grisly," though all that was left were a few shattered bones and some old blood stains. But it amazed Stuart how much of Madeline's final adventure those sharp forensic scientists could actually piece together with just those scraps of damaged evidence. They knew it was Madeline, for instance, and they even figured out his creative use of the miter saw. That was clever.

Thank goodness, they couldn't piece together the motive or the culprit, Stuart said to himself now and again. They just blamed it on a serial killer who was just starting his career around the time Maddie vanished. The mere killing of sweet, innocent Maddie enraged the jury enough to opt for the death penalty. This gladdened Stuart: at least her death got scum like that off the street. His mother and three sisters lived nearby and the killings terrified them. Thanks to Maddie's death, they could finally live without fear of being that beast's next victim.

But Maddie's demise had so many other benefits, too. When the news of her disappearance spread, several companies who wanted to avoid bad publicity by seeming callous and corporately disloyal, renewed their accounts. Since Maddie was gone, Stuart was put in charge and brighter days began. Grundman stayed on for another two years, before retiring. Stuart was promoted and replaced Grundman. Now everyone could be happy. Stuart was a far more lenient boss during the daytime; so that everyone could concentrate on their own burgeoning business.

And that new business could now take off and blossom with an extra dose of care and concentration. Phil could finally retire early, and fulfill his lifelong dream of puttering without the pretense of working. Sally could finally afford a nose job and implants, which helped her in her quest of landing herself a middle-aged former soap actor for a husband. She became semi-retired from the business, but with her house becoming a revolving door of who was who, the business reached new heights.

As for Maddie's legacy, it quickly waned. Though her cherubic face was featured on every news show, magazine, and newspaper (let alone all those victim's rights and death penalty advocates' websites and pamphlets), her popularity cooled after the trial. Yes, there were one or two cable shows and true crime novels that made reference to her sad end, but no legislation bearing her name passed, nor was there any lasting tribute made. Since she had no living relatives, there was no one to carry on her memory.

Everything fell into place and – once again – life became happy for everyone.

All thanks to the death of a footnote.

Snakes Eat Mice Raw

I

Recorded January 16, 2006 9:25 am.

KEATON-ROBERTS MAILBOX: You have reached the voice mail of Audrey Keaton-Roberts. Audrey will away from the office this week, and not be able to respond directly until she gets back. If this is an emergency, please contact Everett Roberts at extension 2555. Thank you.

MAXWELL: Audrey, Joel here. I know you're checking in, and I can't reach you by cell. Call me. We need to talk.

END CALL

II

Subject: Re: Urgent Request for Conference Call
Date: 16/01/2006
From: andre_moretta@keaton-roberts.com
To: s.stone@psycfit.com

Dear Mr. Stone:

I apologize profusely for the delay in responding. Ms. Keaton-Roberts has been called away on an urgent business matter and has not been able to attend to her regular appointments. Please, be assured that this situation is very temporary. Your business is valuable to us and that we are making every effort to ensure you receive the highest level of care that you have come to expect from Keaton-Roberts.

I have gone over your files with Everett Roberts, and he assures me that he will be getting in contact with you personally as soon as possible to set up a conference call regarding changes to the Psycfit account.

Again, my sincerest apologies for any inconvenience this unforeseeable and unavoidable situation may have caused you. We hope to resolve these circumstances to your satisfaction as soon as possible.

Sincerely,

Andre Moretta
Director Client Relations
Keaton-Roberts Statistical Standards Inc.

III

Subject: Greetings from Hell
Date: 16/01/2006
From: andre_moretta@keaton-roberts.com
To: spangledspider@zoomsonic.com

Dude --

Sorry I couldn't get back to you last week – we've had some --
ahem -- crisis management issues and had to pull overtime.
Ingrates didn't even say thanks.

Boss Lady stormed out of the office on Friday, after having a
screeching match with Boss Husband and lost. You should have
seen the chick lose her temper when the guy finally put his foot
down. Woo! Princess of Power got dethroned and crashed on
her rock solid ass. Ugly, ugly. And now she's throwing a big ass
tantrum and not showing up to work. If I did that, I'd be fired so
fast (and actually be a free man), but Her Majesty can do whatever evil she wants.

Now, the clients are all p.o.'d because they can't get in touch
with the Vampire Vixen. Mr. Vixen's been telling everybody
that she's off on an emergency business trip. At least the peons
around here are only going to get flogged by one master instead
of two.

Gotta go – wouldn't want Nick Scratch to catch me wasting
valuable company seconds trying to communicate with the outside world. Catch you later.

A.

IV

Recorded January 23, 2006 11:37 am.

KEATON-ROBERTS MAILBOX: You have reached the voice mail of Audrey Keaton-Roberts. I am either away from my desk or on the phone with another client. Please, leave your name, title, company name, phone number, and a message, and I will get back to you. If this is an emergency, please contact Everett Roberts at extension 2555. Thank you for your call.

MAXWELL: Audrey, you can't keep avoiding me. Sooner or later you are going to have to deal with it. Let's meet for lunch. Call me.

END CALL
*

Recorded January 23, 2006 11:41 am.

ROBERTS MAILBOX: You have reached the voice mail of Everett Roberts, Chief Operating Officer of Keaton Roberts Statistical Standards. I am not here to take your call. Please, leave your name, number, and a brief message and someone will get back to you. If this is an emergency, please contact Audrey Keaton-Roberts at extension 2556. Thank you for choosing Keaton Roberts Statistical Standards.

MAXWELL: Everett, Joel Maxwell here. I can't seem to get in touch with you or Audrey lately. I need to talk to you about an urgent matter. You can reach me on my cell at 746 2527. And don't take today's less-than-spectacular session too seriously -- most companies would kill for your earnings, but you guys were always a cut above the rest. Better luck next time. Thanks.

END CALL

V

Subject: 911 -- Next Steps
Date: 24/01/2006
From: Everett_roberts@keaton-roberts.com
To: Audrey_keaton-roberts@keaton-roberts.com

Audrey

This isn't working for me. I shouldn't have to try to contact you through email of all things. Let's call a truce. We need to devise a plan to get this company – and us – back on the track. I've made reservations at our usual haunt for 8 pm. We need to hunker down as the dynamic duo again.

Rett
*
Subject: Re: 911 -- Next Steps
Date: 24/01/2006
From: Audrey_keaton-roberts@keaton-roberts.com
To: Everett_roberts@keaton-roberts.com

Rett,

I couldn't agree with you more. I don't think we're doing ourselves any favors by avoiding the situation at the company or at home. I have an idea how to set both our spheres right. Dinner it is.

Audrey.

VI
Memorandum   **Confidential**

To: Everett Roberts   **From:**
       Jay Huang-O'Hurley

Date: February 3, 2006
Ref: Proposal to acquire new holdings

Summary Statement: I propose that we not acquire any new domestic or foreign holdings at this time. With changes and instability in the current marketplace, it is best to delay any new acquisitions until the market stabilizes and corrects itself.

VII

Recorded February 7, 2006 7:05 am.

KEATON-ROBERTS MAILBOX: You have reached the voice mail of Audrey Keaton-Roberts. I am either away from my desk or on the on the phone with another client. Please, leave your name, title, company name, phone number, and a message, and I will get back to you. If this is an emergency, please contact Everett Roberts at extension 2555. Thank you for your call.

MAXWELL: Audrey, you are not helping yourself by avoiding my calls. Sooner or later, you are going to have to face everything. If I don't hear from you by the end of the day, I'll just have to pay Everett a nice little visit. Call me.

VIII
Keaton-Roberts Announce Plans to Takeover Statistical Matrixes

Merger would create world's largest commercial testing corporation

BOSTON STAR,   09-02-2006

Dylan Kent, Business reporter

BOSTON, M.A. – Keaton-Roberts Statistical Standards, Inc. the country's largest commercial statistical testing firm is reportedly proposing to make a bid for Britain's Statistical Matrixes, thus forming the world's largest testing company. Numerous reports indicated the maverick company is already in all-night negotiations about a possible merger.

President Audrey Keaton-Roberts and CEO Everett Roberts declined to comment on the reports. Bonnie Carrick, spokeswoman for Statistical Matrixes, also refused comment.

Rumors of the proposed merger sent Keaton-Roberts stock soaring seven per cent, to their highest level since December 2005.

Page 2…

IX

Subject: Stat Mat Negotiations, Phase One
Date: 09/02/2006
From: Audrey_keaton-roberts@keaton-roberts.com
To: Everett_roberts@keaton-roberts.com

Rett,

Things are progressing beautifully. I think the Stat Mat merger
should be only the beginning: we can't afford not to acquire Bio
Stat – it would give us a decisive edge over everyone. I don't
want anyone else to have it. It's a solid outfit that would nicely
address the issues some shareholders have expressed about K-R.

I know we're moving extremely fast, but with everything falling
into place so perfectly, I don't see the reason to hold back our
desire to expand our operations. Let's talk about it over dinner
tonight.

Audrey.
*
Subject: Re: Stat Mat Negotiations, Phase One
Date: 07/02/2006
From: Everett_roberts@keaton-roberts.com
To: Audrey_keaton-roberts@keaton-roberts.com

Audrey

I couldn't agree more with you about getting our hands on Bio
Stat ASAP, but I think we also need to look at acquiring some
other properties that would expand our operations into other
areas. The Stat Mat negotiations have given me quite the appetite in a few other departments, too. Looking forward to this
evening.
Rett

X
Recorded February 23, 2006 10:22 am.

KEATON-ROBERTS MAILBOX: You have reached the voice mail of Audrey Keaton-Roberts. I am either away from my desk or on the on the phone with another client. Please, leave your name, title, company name, phone number, and a message, and I will get back to you. If this is an emergency, please contact Everett Roberts at extension 2555. Thank you for your call.

MAXWELL: Audrey, you are not making me a very happy man. Having your security escorting me out your offices last week, was not the brightest move you've made. Are you screening his business calls, too? I shouldn't have to be slithering around, hunting you down. All I have to do is call Everett on his cell, or meet up with him at his favorite restaurant and everything comes out. Do I make myself clear?

Now, about your proposed little takeover: What the hell are you thinking? You damn well know how much stock I own in Stat-Mat. I strongly recommend you back off or Everett gets drawn a diagram. Snakes eat mice raw, darling.
*
Subject: Re: Still alive A-Man?
Date: 23/02/2006
From: andre_moretta@keaton-roberts.com
To: spangledspider@zoomsonic.com

Dude –

Yeah, I'd love to get back to you, but I am a lowly worker slave toiling in the bowels of hell. Nick and Nikki Scratch are working us overtime so they can torture even more people by making their kingdom bigger. The rich and their twisted ways.

Of course this means everyone has to work eighteen-hour days to make sure this deal goes through. I have no time to take a leak! I have to take calls on my cell as I'm pissing in the bathroom! If the clients knew, they'd freak. Janice had the stomach flu; so, guess what she was doing? Isn't that sad? And you wanted me to get you a job here.

Now the co-dictators are all over each other again. Just like the good old days, when they were too busy making out to whip and torture the underlings. Their business only kicks ass if they're grabbing each others' asses. They never taught us that at businesspeople's school.

Something weird happened – Joel (my old boss and former personal bootlicker to the Bondage Queen herself – before he got a bitching job somewhere else and escaped) called me. He actually remembered someone here besides his old slave driverette, if you can believe it. He asked me if I had Lord Evil's personal cell phone number. Says he wants to ask for his old job back, but doesn't want to do it through Audrey. The chump must be really hard up. Who wants to come back to work here? I had the number; but I wouldn't give it to him until he coughed up something in return. He has the number and now I have tickets to the Demon's Venom concert. I'm a kick-ass negotiator.

I figure once the companies merge, I'll be considered redundant and get my hairy ass fired; so then I'll have all the free time to go clubbing and get trashed. Catch you later.

A.

XI

Subject: Stat Mat Negotiations, Phase Two
Date: 24/02/2006
From: Audrey_keaton-roberts@keaton-roberts.com
To: Everett_roberts@keaton-roberts.com

Rett,

The financial projections look good, and the optics of the deal look even better. We should really push this as hard as we can so that we can attend to other things this evening. Really looking forward to seeing you tonight. I'm ready for some fireworks.

Audrey.

Subject: Re: Stat Mat Negotiations, Phase Two
Date: 24/02/2006
From: Everett_roberts@keaton-roberts.com
To: Audrey_keaton-roberts@keaton-roberts.com

Audrey

In that case, you won't be disappointed. It will be a quite a spectacular scene tonight, let me assure you. I'm ready for some fireworks, too.

Rett.

XII
Destruction of the Fittest: How the Ultimate Power Couple got Devoured by their Prey

Newsmakers Magazine, March 3, 2006

Graham G. Grossman, Business Reporter

Boston, MA – The sleek, bright and open, white corridor at the entrance of Keaton-Roberts Statistical Standards seemed to symbolize the freedom and grandeur that the commercial testing company wanted to embody. "We always thought of those corridors as open and safe," says one employee. "It made us think we were on solid footing, because we were the best and the strongest company in the field. Our possibilities seemed endless here from the moment we stepped into work each morning until the time we walked out of here every night."

However, the inside workings and shenanigans were far darker and more foreboding than outsiders or even many insiders knew. Everett Roberts, founder and CEO filed for divorce this week after details of an extramarital affair between his wife Audrey Keaton-Roberts and Joel Maxwell, a one-time Keaton-Roberts employee were revealed. Maxwell alleges that Keaton-Roberts had allegedly tried to buy his silence about the affair by, among other perks, giving him shares in Statistical Matrixes — the British company which Keaton-Roberts would eventually propose to take over less than a month later.

"If she tried to buy his silence, she certainly was arrogant and careless about the whole thing," says one Keaton-Roberts insider who asked not to be identified. "Joel was a player and he was bound to get more brazen in his demands. [Taking over Statistical Matrixes] may have been a way for Audrey to intimidate Joel and show him she was still boss, but I'm sure he felt threatened and attacked."

News of the divorce sent Keaton-Roberts' stock to plunge seventy-five percent, and many analysts are wondering whether a company that was marketed as being driven by the ultimate corporate-power couple can survive the blow. "Keaton-Roberts was branded as a company {that was} run by two brilliant and focused minds that worked together as one. Now that stockholders and clients have discovered that those brilliant minds are anything but focused or working together, they may write the company off entirely," notes Malcolm Foster, a vice president at HBA Consultants in New York.

Though the husband and wife team stressed their togetherness in the press and famously in their annual reports, many employees were aware of the volatile outbursts between them. "It wasn't a total shock," says one high-level employee who asked not to be identified. "Audrey and Rett had their share of office blowouts; so one figured their marriage wasn't what they pretended it to be. But, lately, the marriage never seemed stronger. They didn't fight at all – Audrey was usually very demanding and expected Rett to be at her beck and call, yet, in the last few weeks, she seemed committed to her marriage. I guess it was a show to keep Rett from suspecting she had an affair and was trying to cover up her tracks."

The couple cultivated their impatient, but unerringly effective reputation by --

Continued on page 22...

XIII
Subject: Re: Paging Doctor Andre
Date: 08/05/2006
From: andretheunemployed@kewlmail.net
To: spangledspider@zoomsonic.com

Dude –

Sorry I couldn't get back to you, but this stupid job-hunting crap is taking up all my free time. Dad was right -- finding a job is a full-time job itself. No job, no cash, no clubbing. I miss my job – at least I had the paycheck, and it wasn't half the work as having to get myself gainfully employed.

It's a cruel, cruel world, my friend. Dog eat dog and all that jazz. So, no partying this weekend for me. Once I find something that resembles work, I'll have all the time and funds to have a grand old time once again, my man. Peace.

A.

Nap Time at the House of Pain

I

"Obviously, we found our old house to be much too small for us. With only four bedrooms, you really can't expect to raise a thriving and gifted young son and daughter in comfort. There was no sunroom, only a modest gazebo and porch, only one dining room, -- and almost no room for the SUV and convertible."

Peggy Ryerson sighed and meticulously and daintily adjusted her cream rose-colored pearl and clear crystal necklace. As she took a bite of her buttered baguette, she discreetly studied her lunch companion's eyes and mouth: did the eyes water and narrow in the right way? Did the jaw drop just low enough or clench just tight enough to confirm feelings of bitter jealousy? Or would Peggy now discuss in detail why she and her husband simply had to upgrade the family car and cottage?

"So, of course, with the new house, we needed a new car that not only wouldn't clash with the façade, but would be practical for our new cottage up north..."

II

"Are you sure you want to go through with this?" The intense young woman asked the question as a matter of insincere courtesy: the red-faced man sitting with clenched fists at the other side of her wooden desk was more than itching for a fight. He wanted to drink the blood of his sworn enemy. Every fiber of his enraged body wanted nothing *but* to go through with it.

So did the young woman in the navy blue skirt and jacket: this would be one profitable venture that would not only produce a delightful fee, but it would enhance to her reputation as being a wunderkind in her field. If the man changed his mind, it meant having to earn that reputation the hard way. She almost regretted phrasing the question that risky way.

"Believe me," began the angry man in the smoky-gray business suit and black tie, "there is nothing more I want, than see those miserable swindlers pay. Ms Carteris, you do what you have to do. I don't care how nasty it gets; I want to make sure the guilty party pays for this. I have other, related matters to attend to."

III

"That shirt is so awesome, Jennie." The young girl with plain brown hair, discount department store sneakers, drug store mango lip balm, and generic, non-designer, gray sweatshirt had generously heaped praise and admiration onto her dainty, well-dressed, and noticeably bored companion for the past five minutes. As they sat in the school cafeteria's uncomfortable chairs, the more fashionable of the two young teenagers seemed unmoved by her companion's raving fashion reviews.

"It's a Sully Seven original," the lithe blonde teenager finally replied with an air of superiority. After all, there was a good chance her less beautiful and refined lunch mate would not know the finer points of teenybopper haute couture.

"It's just so pretty! Baby-blue really looks great on you!"

"That's what the fashion consultant said. Mom takes me to one every season," Jennie sighed and began to eat her homemade lunch: Scottish smoked salmon with low-fat cream cheese served on organic seven-grain bread. Her acquaintance took out her own lunch: peanut butter and jelly on white store-bought bread.

"Ugh," Jennie moaned as she made a face of disgust, "how can you eat *that* bread? It tastes like cardboard."

"But I hate the gross weird-grain stuff you eat…"

"I eat quality foods, Tori," Jennie snapped. "My system can't take all the chemicals they put in common supermarket products. I break out from it!" she added and shook her head, making no attempt at hiding her annoyance.

Tori truly was nothing more than an unpolished and hopeless peasant girl, Jennie thought, drinking her organic peach-and-mango juice. A complete rube with no social skills or status. In fact, if Tori didn't do all of Jennie's homework assignments for her, she'd have absolutely no use for her.

The conversation about bread was suddenly interrupted by the shouts of another young girl who was somewhat more fashionable and comely than Tori. "Bonjour, mes amies!" It was Shannon, one of the girls taking the same French class as Jennie and Tori. "Mangez-vous les sandwichs? Mangez-vous les pains?"

"Knock it off, Shannon," Jennie demanded, rolling her eyes, "I really don't want listen to anymore basic French than I absolutely have to."

"How's it goin', Shannon?" Tori interrupted.

"Great! Just found out we're going to France for the summer break. I'm so excited!"

"That rocks, Shannon, you are so lucky," Tori replied as she began to eat her sandwich.

"I can't wait to go. We're going to Paris, Cannes, and Lyon. I can't believe it!"

"I'm so happy for you. Isn't that cool, Jennie? Have you ever been to France before?"

Jennie just pouted silently in her seat.

IV

"Pressing charges is just the beginning," the man in the suit explained to the investigator and prosecutor sitting with him in the room, "I will cooperate fully with the DA's office. Whatever documents you need, whatever information required is at your disposal. I can't believe what a blind fool I've been. He looked trustworthy and successful -- the pillar of competency and responsibility. Everything I thought was a sign of a good businessman, turned out to be the sign of a con artist and thief. I hope you throw the book at him. It's the least that should happen to someone who's been misusing my books by cooking them."

V

The hallways at Garrison Junior High were always noisy and somewhat odorous, but for most of the students forced to spend a significant portion of their lives there, the noise and the smells were hardly noticeable. There was gossip, primitive flirting, rude insults, and other more important stimulation to keep the pre-teen set occupied.

"Hiya, Jonathan. What are you doing with that cell phone?" one young boy asked his companion who was busy fiddling with his cell phone with seemingly no particular purpose in mind. But, the well-dressed boy ignored his friend.

"Hey, Ryerson, I asked: 'What are you doing with that cell phone'? Cuz you look like you're feeling it up or something!'" The young man snickered at his own attempt at juvenile sexual innuendo. His friend merely frowned and shook his head.

"This stupid cell phone is a pain in the ass! Every time I try to send a message, it goes dead on me. I don't get it; this thing cost a fortune. Top of the line and everything. It's fully loaded with a leather carrying case, and everything else is fine, except the stupid messaging!"

"Yeah," said his friend, nodding in sympathy, "but that one is last year's model. This one just came out. It's way better than yours and it doesn't get messed up when you're messaging." The boy took out his new cell phone and showed it to his friend.

The holder of the older model quickly turned his back on him and stormed away.

VI

Sooner or later, Darren Ryerson was going to have to cut his losses and run as far as his well-shod feet could take him. He knew he couldn't keep the scheme running forever; in fact, he was surprised he pulled it off for this long. He needed more money than he could earn; so he borrowed it from the company he worked for – it wasn't the first or second, or even third company where he helped himself to a share of the pie, but now Darren's gut told him he would need to go elsewhere to finance his family's enviable lifestyle.

Not that his creative bookkeeping was keeping the Ryerson lifestyle afloat completely. The bills were still piling up at an increasingly alarming rate. With so many trinkets and gadgets and toys and baubles becoming more accessible to the common folk, getting a one-up on them wasn't the way it used to be. Keeping up the illusion of wealth wasn't cheap.

Some sacrifices had to be made in the name of making the neighbors, ex-flames, childhood bullies, and rival siblings insanely jealous. The house was rented and all the cars were leased. The credit card bills were choking, as were the phone bills. Everyone needed the latest shirt or the latest phone, or the latest car. His wife Peggy was a high-maintenance woman. So were his children Jennie and Jonathan. And the family dog Peaches.

Yet, there were perks to be had: the house may have been rented, but the evening gown his wife wore was hers, at least, until she returned it to the department store and demanded a refund the next day. Darren's various golf clubs and tennis rackets were all his, at least, until he could pawn them off on an online auction site. It was fair: enjoy the spoils of your exploits until they are no longer needed; sell them, and get more modern spoils to enjoy, until the new season's offerings come up again.

It might have been easier if the Ryersons had opted for more modest accommodations, or at least, comma if Peggy had chosen to put her two university degrees to good use at a well-paying job but then, no one would be begrudgingly impressed. Besides, Peggy insisted on being a stay-at-home yummy mommy – it was more enviable to be a woman who could live the highlife without having to hold an actual job, than to be a woman who had to earn her own keep with her six-figure salary. The rules of the wealthy were always strange to Darren who had a hopelessly middle class mentality. Thank goodness Peggy understood them and could devise their schemes accordingly.

Not that the scheme was all bad and scary. There was too much fun to be had: golfing in Scotland; savoring culinary delights in France; looking hip and learned while in various places in Britain; and doing whatever tourists do in Sardinia. Mind you, Darren had not had the pleasure of experiencing any of that yet, but if he played his cards right, getting to brag about being in Sardinia was a real possibility. But, right now, he had other fish to fry.

Perhaps he could go on helping himself to company funds for another six months – a year at best. That would give him just enough time to find a job at another company, where he could continue to take out secret, forgivable loans for himself. Finding a company that could miss as much money as he needed – and could still offer him a prestigious-sounding title – wasn't an easy task. There had to be a lot of research and casing done before picking the right place of employment – then, he had to actually get the right job in the company. None of that was easy or quick. Earning enough bread to live the dream was always a challenge, no matter how much money Darren could grab from his company.

The thought of having to start over made him uneasy—he almost liked his current job. The only real stress was the fear of getting caught; the actual job was quite pleasant as were his co-workers. Even his employer was a pretty easygoing fellow. No, it wasn't the job that gave him his ulcers or his male pattern baldness.

It was keeping up the lifestyle that was crushing him under its own, formidable, unforgiving weight. The letters he received in the mail were hardly reassuring. Perhaps he could stave off the vultures for a few more months, but only if the Ryersons could cut back a little in the short term. Everything would work out just fine if everyone played their cards right.

VII

"Do you think they have enough for a conviction?" the young assistant asked, walking alongside his employer.

"He was careful, and the paper trail is complicated, but yes, I think there's enough to nail the cheating bastard."

"How much did he embezzle, anyway?"

"I suspect tens of thousands from this company."

The young man whistled as he eyes widen. "That's a pretty penny."

"It certainly is. He was proficient. I suspect he did the same thing to all the other company's he worked for. I've notified all of them about it, and they're all looking into it. He would have been sloppier back then." The man in the suit paused. "No, he can't wiggle out of this one."

"I always wondered how he could afford all those skiing trips and expensive cars and suits. I guess now we know."

The man in the suit grunted and began to walk faster, trying hard to suppress his growing rage.

VIII

"Darren, we have to move to a bigger house – now! And we need a new car. It's already two years old."

"Peggy…"

"Don't 'Peggy' me! Do you realize what a horrible day I had? We need a bigger house!"

"Look, we can't pull another move or another house just yet. I'm going to have to leave the company within the year anyway, so we're going to get another house then…"

"That's not good enough! People are starting to see our house as common! We need something newer and bigger this time…"

"We can't afford it, Peggy! We're drowning in debt. We can't breathe!"

"And I can't breathe knowing everyone's looking down on me."

"I don't owe you a princess lifestyle. You want a bigger house? Go get a job and earn it!"

"Absolutely not! What would people think if I got a job now? They'd think we were broke."

"We *are* broke – and getting more broke by the minute. We're lucky if we don't get evicted by the end of the year…"

The arguing was halted by the sudden opening of the door. It was Jennie, looking distinctly upset and humiliated.

"What's the matter, Jennie?" Darren asked.

"Dad, Shannon and her parents are going to France. I have to go France *and* Sweden, too…"

"We'll talk about it some other time…"

"But nobody's talking about my Sully Seven shirt anymore…"

"We can't afford an expensive trip like that right now…"

Peggy threw back her head. "This family has never gone on a decent vacation since Australia – and how long ago was that?"

"We can't afford a trip and we can't afford another move to a house with more rent. Don't you understand, Peggy? Our backs are up against the wall! I can't take the collector's phone calls or their threatening letters anymore!"

"It's not fair. Shannon's family gets to go to France. Why can't we go to France, too?"

"Because we can't afford a trip and your clothes and your gadgets and your lessons all at once. Something has to give."

"Dad! I have to get a new cell phone. Everyone's making fun of mine. It's not good enough," a whiny Jonathan replied, sulking, as he came into the living room.

The only thing Darren wanted was an escape from his long, waking slumber. Anywhere, anyplace that wasn't this terrible house where everyone – mother, father, and children, were nothing more than well-dressed vultures.

There was a knock on the door. Darren bolted from the living room and opened the front door. Two police officers were standing in front of him.

"Darren Ryerson?"

With a sigh of relief, Darren nodded and let the police officers into the house. He knew within a matter of seconds, he would no longer have to worry about scoring a bigger house, car, cottage, trip, or cell phone. It was the worst relief imaginable but now at least, he could finally breathe and feel awake again.

Buy Me Something!

I

October drizzle was never pleasant, but combined with the crisp, sturdy winds and the matte, smoky sky it all confirmed the painfully obvious: an early, unpleasant winter. That realization lead to many more: boots, hats, mitts, coats and snow pants would have to be purchased for the eldest ones as soon as possible. The extra layers would be another annoying expense to consider while standing outside the toy store waiting for the staff to open its glass doors.

The large, restless mob of vexed stay-at-mall moms was already impatiently peering inside at the seemingly lackadaisical staff, hoping the workers would show some pity toward the shivering crowd and grant an early entrance into the store. There were cold, vulnerable children to think about: children who could get sick, distressed or worse, loud and weepy. The frigid and pricking rain made the time seem to go by more slowly. The sales associates seemed comfortable and warm indoors, even if they were wearing their colorful short-sleeved shirts. They were in no hurry to let the first crush of antsy, peeved, and sniffling customers into their serene little world.

The mothers waiting in the cold began to complain out loud. The drizzle was turning into rain, and in their baggy sweatpants and dark, half-zipped windbreaker jackets, the women were no match for the stout elements they faced. Their heads of unkempt, windblown hair and sour, lined faces fully confessed their anger and bitterness at being forced to wait for someone inside to just get off his lazy duff to turn a simple lock.

The unsheltered adults made no attempt to hide their disappointment, anxiousness, and fatigue. Some leaned on their shopping carts, while others attempted to make eye contact with the staff and then point at their watches. Why could the staff not open their doors a mere fifteen minutes early? The customers were in a hurry, after all. It didn't help matters that it was a Professional Development Day and that their children had the day off school.

The uneasiness of the mothers quickly spread to their offspring, though the taunting weather and the teasing toys inside had made their chattering children weepy and desperate. The joy of missing school and going to the toy store had already been forgotten. Few could keep their thoughts to themselves:

"Mom! Why can't we wait in the car? I'm freezing."

"*Ah-choo!*"

"I want a Train Boy…"

"Can I have a Daffy Dilton? Please?"

"You know you can't have one."

"*Ah-choo!*"

"Why not?"

"Come back here, buddy. I don't want to have to be chasing you all over the parking lot. Did you hear me, bud? Get back here now!"

"I'm freezing…"

"I wanna go back in the car…"

"Now!"

"Aww, it's too cold. Why did we have to come so early, anyway?"

"If you don't behave, we're going home. I mean it! Come back here, Joshua. Come back here now! Joshua, did you hear me? Joshua!"

"I'm going in the car."

"No, you're not. You don't even have the key. Now get back here!"

"I have a sore throat, mommy."

Fourteen more minutes to go.

It would be a long wait.

II

"Good morning, Toy Empire shoppers. The store is now open."
The perky, garbled message was barely audible, but the moment
one gangly employee sauntered over to the entrance and
unlocked the door, the mob savored the announcement as they
pushed the young man aside and ran inside the store. The bang-
ing of shopping carts drowned out most of the other pager an-
nouncements. It was time to get to work.

"Mom," one eight year old boy began, walking and playing his
hand-held video game at the same time, "Can I buy a new game
for my e-Matrix?"

His mother frowned and shook her head abruptly. "You know
you can't have another game. You already have five. We came
to buy a present for your cousin's birthday."

"Please?"

"No! Now what do you think she'd like? A barbie doll?" It was
almost a rhetorical question: dolls were the least expensive of the
girl's toys and the easiest of presents to buy. It would be a nice,
easy purchase, and then it would be off to the department store
to look at the silk flowers and the garbage bags.

"Susie doesn't like barbies," the young man blurted, surprised
that his mother did not know what his cousin liked.

"All girls like barbies," his mother replied patronizingly, trying
hard to suppress her panic at the thought of spending more than
eight dollars for the gift.

"She hates barbies! She likes model trains."

"She does not!"

180

"Yes, she does! Her whole room has nothing but trains; even her wallpaper has trains, and her bed is shaped like a train."

"Well, I'm not spending that kind of money on her. We're buying her a barbie."

"But she hates barbies!" The young man grabbed his mother by her dry hand and began to tug her toward the train section.

"We're *not* buying her a train. That's too expensive."

"But, they're on sale! Look!" The young man pointed to the endcap that was stacked with bright red and blue toy trains. On top of the top shelf there was a sign that declared the goods to be seventy-five per cent less than the original price.

"OK, buddy," his mother conceded as she looked at the price and nodded, "we'll buy her this."

"Susie's gonna like that," the young man said triumphantly. Then he paused and as his mother took one of the trains and put it in her shopping cart he added, "I found Susie's present. Does that mean I can have a new game?"

"No."

"Oh, come on! I promise I won't ask for another…"

"No."

"Even if I get an 'A' on my math test?"

"Stop it!"

"And my science test?"

His mother began to briskly head for the checkout line.

"We're going ... now!"

"I'll do the dishes for a whole month…"

"Stop it!"

"It's not fair. I found Susie's present."

"We're leaving the store."

"And I'll keep my room clean. I promise I won't ask for another game. It's not fair! Susie gets a present…"

III

Next to cars and bricks, homely and deformed action figures were a boy's true love. The sicklier the skin color, the more attractive it became. Multiple limbs and eyes were also a positive feature, as were fangs, scaly skin, braided muscles, and massive weapons. If the action figure made noise or oozed, then it would be a virtual guarantee that the boy in question would forever cherish his sacred plastic god.

It was one such blister-packaged deities, appropriately named "Disguss T'orr" that caught the fancy of six swooning brothers as they stared with reverence, while wiping their noses with the back of their sticky hands.

Their heavy-set mother, sensing an impeding request, tried to cut it off at the pass.

"Put it on your list, boys, and maybe Santa will get it for you on Christmas."

"But it's Disgusthor, mommy," the four-year-old helpfully explained as he hopped in place. "He fights the bad guys!"

"Yeah," the five-year-old piped in as he pulled his underwear out of inconvenient places. "He fights crime with his Berp-a-laser!"

"I want Disgusthor," the four-year-old interrupted; his hopping became increasingly animated.

"Me, too," added the six-year-old. "He's so cool! Can we have him? Please?"

"Please?" the other five brothers pleaded in unison.

"His gas bombs are awesome," the nine-year-old noted and his seven-year-old brother nodded, touching one of the coveted toys.

"Joshua," his mother started.

"And when you squeeze him, his Green Goo of Justice comes out of his nose," the eight-year-old shouted with glee.

The sudden outburst of giggling from the boys startled the other shoppers.

The boys quickly looked at their mother.

"Please?" they repeated in unison.

"Just put it on your list, boys, and maybe Santa will bring it on Christmas."

"Thanta neva bwings toyths! He bwings underweaw," blurted the four-year-old angrily as he stomped his foot in protest.

"Yeah," yelled the other ones in show solidarity.

"I'm not buying you that now."

The six boys quickly surrounded their mother and looked at her with pleading eyes.

"Please?"

"We never ask for underwear!"

"Santa never listens."

"He never brings us toys."

"Thanta Cwas hates us."

"Please?"

"I'm sure Santa will bring it if you all ask him nicely. Come on, let's go." The woman held on to the shopping cart tightly and quickly pushed the cart to the girls' arts and crafts section.

IV

"Train Boy, Mama, I wanna Train Boy!" the three- year-old pajama-clad boy chirped from his seat in the shopping cart as he pointed to the large display of various Train Boy toys: Train Boy preschool dolls, Train Boy puzzles, Train Boy stack-up bricks, and Train Boy trains with plastic tracks.

"You can't have a Train Boy. You have lots of toys at home," his mother replied as sweetly as she could, while scouring the store for the preschool book section. It was most unfortunate that her ignorance of the floor plan and the lack of visible staff lead her straight to her young son's cartoon idol.

"I wanna Train Boy," the young boy began to sniffle; his eyes turn red and watery.

"Come on, buddy, we're here to buy your new little friend a present, ok?" she replied slowly and brightly.

"But I wanna Train Booooooooooooooooooooy," the child replied and he began to cry.

"You can't have a Train Boy," she said more firmly. "Some other time, bud. Not now. Let's go buy a book for your friend."

"But I wanna Train Bo-o-o-o-y!"

"If you don't stop crying, we are going home!"

"I wanna Train Boy," her son whined as he tried to hold back his tears.

"We're going to go home. I mean it!"

The child began to wail. "Waaaaaaaaaaaaah!"

"You're being a bad boy! We're going to go home if this continues."

"Waaaaaaaaaaaaaaaaaah!"

His mother sighed, turned her cart around and headed for the next aisle. Perhaps she could find what she was looking for over there.

"Train Booooooooooooooooooooooooooooy!
Waaaaaaaaaaaaaaaaaaaaah! Train
Booooooooooooooooooooooooooooooy!"

V

A ten-year-old boy was looking breathlessly at the wall of toys cars, while adjusting his baseball cap. His mother caught a glimpse of his view, and shook her head. "Come on, buddy, let's go."

"Awww, but I want a new toy."

"We're here to buy something for your aunt's baby shower."

"Can't I have a toy car?"

"No."

"But they're only fifty cents!"

"Absolutely not! I'm not going to be spending that kind of money on frivolous nonsense."

"But I have a dollar!"

"Sorry, buddy, not today."

"But why not?"

"I told you. We do not make those kinds of purchases."

"But you bought perfume and two-hundred-dollar shoes yester-day!"

"That's different."

"Is that why you hid it from dad?"

"Young man, don't you dare talk like that to your mother!"

"I don't know why you can buy things, but I can't."

"I buy things I need."

"Did you need all those necklaces you bought last week?"

"As a matter of fact, I did. If you do not want to get grounded, you will keep quiet."

"Does dad know you bought all those bed sheets?"

"It's not a dad's job to know about things like that! Now let's buy that stroller and get out of here. Mommy has to go to the mall to buy herself some red stiletto shoes."

VI

"Doesn't anyone work here?" the young woman asked herself shrilly as she held her six-year-old daughter's hand tightly.

"I want a Daffy Dilton," the young girl shouted playfully as she pointed to the doll section.

"Not today, honey. We have to buy something for daddy! You know how he likes to collect his action figures," her mother explained with a hint of disgust in her voice.

"But I want a Daffy Dilton!" Her daughter pouted as she stomped her foot.

"Piper…"

"Daddy always gets all the toys!" The young girl began to cry.

"Piper!"

"I want a Daffy Dilton," Piper screamed. Her face turned red and she defiantly clenched her fists.

"Piper! You stop that tantrum this instant!"

But Piper continued her feral rage unabated. She yelled as she threw herself on the floor and flailed her arms and legs.

"Piper!"

"Nooooooooooooooooo…"

"Piper, get off the floor now!"

"Nooooooooooooooooooo!"

"Piper! We are going to leave this instant if you don't get up from that floor."

"Nooooooooooooooooooooo!"

The young woman tried to lift her daughter, but the girl's continual kicking and flailing made the task a painful one. A slap on the arm here; a kick in the shin there. The woman's face turned red. "That bastard can buy his own damned toys."

Grabbing one of her daughter's legs, the woman dragged the screaming girl out of the store.

As the woman came outside, the cold wind and relentless rain immediately reminded her of her earlier unpleasantness. Feeling the rain on her face, the screaming young girl yanked her leg to free herself from her mother's grasp, and quickly jumped to her feet, still sniffling and crying.

Her mother adjusted her own jacket, grabbed her daughter's hand, and ran to her car.

There was another store to visit.

After all, it was barely eleven in the morning.

War-Torn Mila

I

It wouldn't be long now before the sounds of tired, upset children, buzzing noises from earphones; tipsy ramblings from fellow passengers and perky stewardess would be silenced and forgotten. This flight had been an unusually stuffy and tedious one, and with passengers and crew alike contributing to the unpleasantness. No one had admired the view from above; instead most passengers would chalk up the flight as unbearable.

There was one passenger who had been oblivious to both the charm and the chaos. Sitting quietly at the back of the plane was a beautiful and slender young woman who would have been even more stunning if she didn't over-pluck her eyebrows, laid off the bleach and perm, and went easy on the white, shiny eye shadow and light-pink lipstick.

Mila looked over her documents out of nervous boredom: her passport was in her hand as was her K-1 visa. The plane would be landing soon enough. The flight from Moscow had not been a direct one, and there had been stopovers and delays, but finally she would be meeting her husband-to-be for the first time.

All she knew was that he was a wealthy American, named Wendell Dubuque, who lived in Wisconsin. Her mother told her that was all that she needed to know and she had taken care of the details and correspondence, lest her daughter botch up the potential pairing as she did with the Canadian. Mila had hoped to get lost in Los Angeles or New York City, but her mother wanted her to marry an American in a smaller state, where there was a better chance of Mila's brother getting accepted in a smaller university. That way, her mother explained, her younger offspring would get more attention and would be seen as being somewhat intriguing and exotic. New York, her mother lectured sternly, could wait.

Lecturing was something Mila's mother did a lot of during the last few months. Grab everything you can grab from America and from life, her mother advised her again and again as Mila packed a small suitcase for her new life abroad. It was her mother who devised the plan that she find an American or Canadian husband, and then – once she got her citizenship – bring the rest of the family over from Moscow. The scheme was in the works since the girl was sixteen. At first, her mother had tried through her own contacts to find Mila a spouse. There were some setbacks that had forced her to change her strategy to get her and her children out of poverty and the country. One Canadian lead looked promising, until the young man's mother got wind of the upcoming nuptials and put a stop to the scheme.

Determination had eventually paid off: thanks to a Russian dating agency and a revealing picture of the shapely Mila in a skimpy bathing suit, she quickly landed herself a prospective husband who had her mother's seal of approval. The finalized plan would be simple enough: stay married for two years until she could get her papers, and then get a divorce. Alimony would tide her over until she could find a better prospect. She would be twenty-two years old, still young enough to enjoy her youth, but old enough to do whatever she wanted.

*　　　　　　　　　　　　*

　　　　　*

The flight and subsequent dealings with customs went as smoothly as Mila had expected. As she now went in search of her fiancé, she took the picture of Dubuque out of her coat pocket and took a look: the young man was plain-looking with not much in the way of distinctive features. Finding Dubuque would not be simple. She began looking at all the young men; which one was the one she would love and honor for the next couple of years? No one seemed to match the picture.

A loud, unnervingly cackling laugh came behind her, startling her. "Dammit, Mila, you too stupid to know your own husband?"

Mila nervously turned around and looked at the man whose booming voice had startled her: he was a rough and tall man, nowhere near as attractive as the man in the photo. He was balding, about fifty, with seemingly no regard to his personal hygiene. His kestrel eyes studied her carefully, even if his laugh suggested he was in a more jovial mood. Tears flowed from Mila's eyes. The picture he sent to her was obviously not his. But, by the looks of him, he most likely wasn't close to being wealthy. Or honest.

Or sane.

Mother, what horrible mess did you get me in, she thought as she tried to stop her hands and lower lip from trembling.

Ignoring her fear, Wendell merely grabbed her by the arm and went to pick up her suitcase. Within days, Mila would become his wife.

II

It was only a month since she arrived from Moscow, and her mother had gotten her more than just a husband. She got her daughter living in a run-down, isolated farm in the middle of nowhere. No neighbors; no stores; no Internet connection; no pipeline to the outside world. This had not been part of the bargain. Her mother was supposed to advise her on her next moves. Now Mila had to think and grab chances for herself.

Though her mother and brother assured her that abusive mail-order husbands were just a myth, she was immediately responsible for the house and farm work his small and cold, dilapidated shack needed. Wendell was a hard, manipulative spouse who, from the start, relished instilling fear into his young new bride.

And he was very good at keeping Mila off balance: the maniac would not allow her to sleep, nor was she allowed to bathe or eat without his approval. She was forbidden to speak at all – not even a "yes" or "no" could come from her lips. Mila had not uttered a word since her marriage at City Hall.

Then came cleaning and feeding Wendell's three insane Dobermans who would be locked up outside in their inhumane and cramped cages. The dogs terrified Mila, though she did her best to try to appease them, by speaking to them in a sweet, but firm voice. She tried hard not to show her fright, but Wendell's booming voice and controlling ways weren't easy to take.

The run-down farm was isolated, and as far as she could tell, miles away from civilization. There was no contact with the outside world: she was forbidden from calling her mother or brother. "Nope," Wendell bellowed the first night he took his bride-to-be home. "I paid for your plane ticket, wedding ring, and service. I'm not wasting another dime on you."
She was alone in a filthy farmhouse with a madman.

This was not part of her mother's master plan.

But Mila had to endure almost two years before she could flee to freedom with her citizenship and be able to grab everything her heart desired.

It was the only comfort that helped ease her mind as she fed the snapping, barking dogs in their rusted cages.

III

"Dammit, woman, wake up! Now!" It was the maniac, shaking Mila out of bed and throwing her on the wooden floor. As she looked around confused, Wendell's chortling made her already fragmented mind scatter further.

"Listen,' Wendell began as he stood over his bride, lightly kicking her naked thigh as she shivered in her underwear, "it's our two-months anniversary and I thought we'd celebrate in style."

Mila's comprehension of English was better than her verbal abilities, but her fatigue and fear made her slow and feeble. The maniac could see her confusion.

"We…are…going…to…have…a…little…fun…today," he shouted slowly as he began to leave the bedroom. "I'm…gonna…be…right…back…"

Mila got up from the floor and was about to put on a bathrobe when Wendell came back, carrying a shotgun.

"Surprise, honey."

Mila froze, her eyes desperately darting around the room, looking for an escape. There was none.

"For our anniversary, I thought we'd play a new game. Keep the marriage alive." He paused, savoring the sight of Mila shivering. "I give you a head start and then we'll see how good of a runner you are. I start firing on the count of ten. Ready?"

Mila ran past Wendell and bolted out the bedroom door.

"*One…*"

Tripping on the carpet she ran through the living room, knocking over a small corner table.

"*Two...*"

Unlocking the front door, the semi-naked young woman ran outside, screaming.

"*Three...*"

There was no place to escape. With no keys, she could not flee by truck. The gates were locked; she could not escape by foot. With no one around for miles, her screams were a wasted investment.

Where to hide? Behind a tree? There was no time to consider her options. She cowered as she heard Wendell open the front door and come outside.

"*Ten!* All right, I'm coming for you! Remember? It's til death do us part..."

The sound of footsteps stopped almost as soon as they started.

"Behind the tree, are ya? Gotcha!"

Wendell aimed his gun at the tree. The first bullet hit an evergreen beside her. The second hit the ground less than inch from her left foot, and triggered a chorus of barking from the Dobermans. The third nearly grazed her right cheek. Mila screamed, and then ducked for cover behind a run-down shed. More bullets were coming close, but never managing to hit the human target. Wendell reloaded, then began firing anew, all the while chasing his prey and whooping and hollering, "Look at that woman run like a rabbit! Come on, bunny, run!"

Everywhere Mila ran, she was met with gunfire. Not only would she die at the hands of a madman in a godforsaken place, but she would never get to the grabbing or living her mother encouraged her to do. There was nowhere else to run; Wendell was catching up to her, cornering her at the back of the house. It was over, she thought, as she turned around and stared her executioner in the eyes.

Wendell aimed his gun straight at Mila's head for a minute, then put it down and laughed.

"Say, that was pretty good! The last one gave up after three minutes; wet herself and grossed me out. At least, you know how to play the game. We'll do this again real soon, honey. All that fun worked me up an appetite. I'll have the usual. Now go inside and make me something to eat."

Wendell walked away.

No, she could not take another game like this. There was only one thing to do: find a way to call Mother and tell her about Wendell -- and that she was going to take the first flight back to Moscow. She tried to gather her courage as she heard the angry dogs bark relentlessly in the background.

IV

Mila unsteadily place the phone back into the cradle. Wendell
was out in the backyard, leaving her alone long enough to call
her mother collect. It was a short and terse call. Her mother
wasn't worried that she had been silent for three months, or that
the she was subject to running for her life in her underwear almost every day. Her mother was quite to the point: You've been
nothing but a disappointment to me. Your brother must attend
an American school and get his papers. You are to endure the
marriage until the time has come.

In other words, Mila was on her own.

The strangeness of it all: her mother saw her as a foot soldier –
the disposable pawn in her own fight for a better life. True, it
was her mother's plan to all but prostitute her only daughter on
another continent without any support or safety, but Mila as-
sumed her mother did that, because she loved her. Mila would
sacrifice for the betterment of her family and the chance to buy
designer dresses, and in return, her small family would be worry-
ing about her well-being back home.

She could not retreat, her mother snapped. Of course, she was
in enemy territory, but that's how wars were fought and won –
in the trenches. Just keep him happy until the time was right.
When INS pays a visit, play the role of the doting wife. Be a
good solider and do as I have instructed you, or your brother
will never get to live the good life. She then hung up.

Things just weren't as complicated as Mila hoped they were,
they were terrifyingly simple. She was being used: by her husband, by her brother, by her mother, and by herself. Mila's comfort was not even a minor consideration.

Of course, she fully went along the scheme, all in the hopes that she, too, could find a way to grab the spoils of war, while she bided her time. But her situation was plain: no one was going to save Mila, but Mila.

She was not going to live to see her first wedding anniversary if she did not plan an escape, and if she did manage to flee, she would be broke, alone, unemployed, vulnerable, homeless, and without a citizenship. She could even be arrested or deported.

It was still a step up to where she was now. The only question was: how was she going to get away from Wendell's clutches?

She could hear the maniac loading his shotgun in the kitchen as he was knocking empty beer bottles on the tiled floor. It meant only one thing: Wendell had come back inside – and it was time for another round of his game.

V

The promise of better things was the root of all stupid decisions, Mila thought as she ran out of the house at the count of one. Where could she hide without being spotted right away? Was it safer on the left of the shed? No, the right side had better cover.

Marriage had to be the most misused concept in the world. Just as much as the maniac used marriage as a way of tormenting another person, Mila misused it to buy more lipstick. Neither had any business exchanging vows, but now...

Breathe, think, and hide, Mila thought to herself as she dodged behind shed to avoid detection. The maniac was drunker than usual. No use: he saw her and repeatedly fired. His aim was more unpredictable, and the number of bullets he was shooting more than usual.

He had grown tired of his quarry. She had seconds to save herself. She had nowhere to go; and no safe place to hide. What she needed was a weapon to defend herself. But what?

Then she remembered: the dogs. The only ones that could save her now were the dogs.

The half-insane Dobermans were vicious and ready to attack anything or nothing, but they liked Mila. She fed them; she talked to them; she refused to show any fear in their presence. She befriended them and gave them affection and more so than the maniac ever did. Would they return the favor and help her in her time of need?

The odds were against her: after all, dogs were loyal beasts and they were Wendell's animals. At worst, the dogs would turn on her, maul her, disfigure her, and possible kill her, and at this point she did not want to die; not here, and not like this.

But how would she save herself, then? She could not overpower him, or reason with him, or even outrun him. There was no escape; the farm was too isolated for her to run away and find help. The dogs were her only chance.

Being careful not to show her position to the maniac, Mila slid down to the ground and as quickly and quietly as she could crawled to the dog cage. As she came close she softly whispered as she smiled at the three dogs, but simultaneously tried to assert a firm and authoritative position. Her reassuring and calm demeanor got the dog's attention and compliance. As Wendell shot another bullet in the air, Mila opened the cage, never ceasing to smile.

The dogs were free. The real test began. Would the dogs turn on her? Would they run away? Or would Wendell manage to take control away from her?

There was no time to think. Just as one of the dogs gently sniffed her, one shot fired in the air. Wendell began to cackle anew. The dogs quickly ran toward the gunshot. Another gunshot roared. Frantic barking a growling of dogs exploded, at the same second a scream pierced the air – it was Wendell's scream.

The dogs wandered out of the yard. Mila stayed on the cold ground for several minutes, too frightened to move, lest the maniac was still well enough to shoot. Shivering, but determined to see the damage, she slowly crawled through the yard until she saw her tormentor's working boot clad feet lying still in the grass. When she was certain he was not going to move, she got up from her hideout and slowly walked over to the body.

The maniac's face was torn and bloody. His nose was mauled off; his neck had a wide-open gash. His hands were marred by defensive wounds.

The shotgun lay only inches away from the body, but just as Mila began to breathe a sigh of relief, she could hear gurgling coming from the maniac.

Wendell wasn't dead.

Not yet, at least.

Carefully avoiding the blood, or getting too close to her husband, Mila leaned over and took a look at the mess on the ground.

"Dammit, you stupid woman, what you done now?" Wendell wheezed as he weakly tried to grab her with his bloody arms. The pain and his blood-stained vision prevented any successful attempt, frustrating him further.

"I'm gonna kill you!"

"I do not think so…"

Wendell ignored her. "Call an ambulance, dammit! I'm gonna bled to death!"

"No ambulance." Mila was full of anger and hate, but she managed to reply in a low, slow voice.

"I said, now! I'm dying…"

"No. No ambulance."

"Listen, you bitch, you call an ambulance right now or I'll blow your head off!"

"No. You die here," Mila said resolutely as she shook her finger at the crumpled figure on the ground. Before the maniac had the chance to grab his shotgun, she kicked it away from her tormentor.

"Now, you fight me."

"Shut up!"

"Fight me now, big man."

Wendell looked desperate. "Listen, bitch, let's make a deal: you call an ambulance, and I won't chase you around the farm no more. Come on, man, I'm dying. Deal?"

"No deal," Mila spat defiantly as she turned her back and walked away. "You will die like pig."

Dammit, he was going to die here in the worst possible way. The maniac's anger was only tempered by his pain and the knowledge he was bested by a cheap little floozy. He was losing consciousness and he knew it. The worst part of all: Mila wouldn't be charged for his murder. His fingerprints were all over gun; the shell casings were all over the backyard; and he was drunk. The police would simply come to the conclusion that Wendell's relentless gun shots frightened his rabid dogs, and they broke free on their own and snapped. It wasn't supposed to end like this: the games at Mila's expense had grown tiresome and he wanted fresh meat to torment.

That ungrateful troublemaker really was going to get the best of him in the end, even if he did hold all the power, cards, and rifles. That just didn't seem fair – just as he had eyed an online profile of a young girl from Thailand who he wanted to replace Mila. But now ... she was going to get everything and get away with everything. The irony was sickening, thought Wendell as looked up at the darkening sky. The last thing he heard as he began to lose consciousness was the sound of his barking Dobermans in the background and Mila running into the house and slamming the door.

VI

Mila sat alone at a café patio during her lunch break and watched the downtown workers rush to their different destinations. Today was an anniversary of sorts for her, and she wanted to quietly celebrate and savor her independence. It was four years since she liberated herself from the maniac's farm.

Things did not turn out as badly as she thought they might: she was neither deported nor arrested. She was detained for awhile by INS, but one look at Wendell's mauled body, empty beer bottles, and fired rifle, and Mila was set free. Fortunately, her tragedy made local news, and there was no shortage of people willing to help a frightened, waif-like young widow who was alone in the world, and was most concerned that the dogs responsible for their owner's demise neither be put down nor abandoned. Mila had pleaded *their* case to rolling cameras, not her own.

One organization took her under their wing and had immediately helped her, eventually helping her get a work permit. The job was fine enough, and shortly after Mila took English classes and managed to find work as a receptionist at a downtown office in Milwaukee. As for her furry saviors, she managed to find a home for each one. It was a fair trade, she thought and turned her attention to the birds that flew into the patio, looking for bread crumbs on the ground.

As for Mother and Brother, they could stay in Moscow to plan their next crusade. Besides, if either one wanted to come to America so badly, they could marry someone like Wendell and live with him themselves.

As the crowd beside the patio grew, then disintegrated, a playful Mila covertly tossed a few bread crumbs to the small bird at her feet and watched it eat. What a small, delicate creature, she thought. Yet, somehow it managed to find its own way and survive the elements and predators, all on its own. The hungry, spry bird finished the bread crumbs, shook its feathers, and then quickly flew away.

U spin me, baby! (*But will it play in PR-ia?*)

Subject: Newest Appointment
Date: 11/04/06
From: president@silverport.edu
To: staff@silverport.edu

Please join us in welcoming Silverport University's latest employee Katrina Norrins in her newly created role as Vice President, Public Relations for Student Affairs.

Katrina brings with her more than twenty years experience in public relations in both the private and public sectors. She has a Bachelor of Arts in Journalism and a Master's degree in Sociology. She has mostly recently worked at the University's Office of Public Relations. Prior to that, she had leadership roles at Williams, Taylor and Fielding Public Relations and worked as a publicist for Truscott and Ashford, a prestigious academic publisher.

Katrina Norrins is an exceptional leader and straightforward communicator with ambitious and innovative ideas for Silverport University and its student body. She believes in the importance of education and will make it her priority to ensure that Silverport students have a strong, active voice in their local media, on campus, and in their community as leaders of tomorrow.

I have every confidence that she will excel in her newly created post, and I am delighted to have the opportunity to work closely with her.

As part of her duties, Katrina will develop and enhance communication ties between students and the media; work with both students and the community; and ensure Silverport University continues to be regarded as one of the nation's most prestigious academic institutions, dedicated to instilling knowledge, decorum, and ethics into the innovators and leaders of the future.

Katrina may be contacted at Katrina_Norrins@silverport.edu and her extension is 2524.

Travis Tanner
President
--

The Silverport Sterling

The Independent Student Voice of Silverport University

Honor Students, Football Team Embroiled in Sex Ring Allegations

11/07/06

Gray Jordan, Staff Reporter

The Orion Police Department is investigating shocking allegations that over a dozen students on the Dean's Honor List were allegedly pressured by Silverport guidance counselors to provide sexual favors and sexually explicit photographs and movies of themselves to the university's football team in exchange for inflated grades and scholarships.

Members of the football team, in turn, were allegedly given incentives to improve their on-field performance in exchange for selecting students they wanted and what specific sexual acts they allegedly wanted performed.

The allegations surfaced after a second-year Drama major filed a report with the Orion police...

More...

--

11-08-06, 2:32 AM   Re: Silverport Sex Ring?
        Post #98

KYJellyboy
Member
Location: in ur pants
Member 214

213

Posts: 38

yeah, all the msm is hyping this
bs already, some ppl need 2 get
a life. it's not like ne1 put a gun
2 those keeners' heads & told
them they had 2 give the football team a blow job & btw, did
u hear, kristi already hired
some kind of pr people 2 rep
her little bitch ass. WTF?

11-08-06, 2:42 AM   Re: Silverport Sex Ring?
Post #99

hOnEyNiNjA7
Advanced Member
Location: Orion
Member 178
Posts: 107

Everyone on campus knows
Kristi is a wannabe starlet and
drama queen. All she does is
brag about *almost* making the
final cut on some fifth-rate cable "reality" show (yeah, like
she knows anything about reality! LOL) I guess even the producers couldn't stomach the
idea of having to put up with
her and sent her home packing.
I bet she's the one who leaked
the allegations to the press so

she could get some free publicity out of it. She already gave
some TV interview today!
TODAY! The girl works fast on
so many levels! LOL!

11-08-06, 2:52 AM   Re: Silverport Sex Ring?
    Post #100

Crash
Starter
Member 347
Posts: 1

I saw the interview. I was really
surprised that someone who
claims to be a victim of that
kind of disgusting abuse would
agree to reveal her face and
identity and give an interview
so fast.

11-08-06, 3:02 AM   Re: Silverport Sex Ring?
    Post #101

KYJellyboy
Member
Location: in ur pants
Member 214
Posts: 38

hey, welcome 2 our 4um, crash!
@honey: u said it! :-P

11-08-06, 3:14 AM   Re: Silverport Sex Ring?
        Post #102

hOnEyNiNjA7
Advanced Member
Location: Orion
Member 178
Posts: 107

Don't I know it, **KY**. Thanks to
Kristi, everyone who has anything above a **B** average in
Drama is looked upon as a
streetwalker. So many of us
have had to get professional
representation: to help us de-
cide which reporters to talk to
and what to say and how to
dress. You wouldn't believe
how many requests for interviews we're getting now. I had
to touch up my roots at the last
minute and had to hit up my
parents to get a new wardrobe.
What a bother!

--

Kristi Bellows
A Chronicle about Living the Dream

November 9, 2006
Blaming the Victim
Mood: Despair

I thought I was doing the right thing when I made my name and face public, but the hurtful, vile things said about me on campus and in the media have been so hard to take.

We all know that most actors and performers start in the business "starving." Well, I am one of the hungry. I needed that scholarship and the pressures to keep it were huge. I was trapped and alone. I was taken advantage of, and I want everyone to know that I am one of the victims here, not the football team or the university. I have been called all sorts of names since I gave that TV interview last night. I am not a gold digger or a liar: I am a VICTIM and more importantly, an aspiring ACTRESS with COMMERCIAL appeal and branding possibilities. But no one seems to understand.

That is why I have hired an agent and public relations firm to handle my publicity. They think a serialized documentary following this police investigation and (hopefully) trial, will vindicate me and help me with my career, since other options have suddenly been taken away from me.

But it's *NOT* about the money or the fame. It's about restoring my good name and finding CLOSURE.

UPDATE: I had to close the comments on my site because too many hurtful sickos were making unfounded and disgusting accusations against me. The sexism in this day and age is shocking.
--

PRESS RELEASE
FOR IMMEDIATE RELEASE
November 9, 2006.

ORION, CA – Silverport University President Travis Tanner announced today that the university is investigating claims about sexual misconduct between Silverport's football team and members of the Dean's Honor List.

"We are fully cooperating with investigators and we are confident that the faculty will be cleared of any wrongdoing," says Katrina Norrins, Vice President, Public Relations for Student Affairs. "Though it is too early in the investigation to gauge the extent of the problem, we will accept full responsibility for any wrongdoing the investigation may find, and we will actively take whatever actions are necessary to ensure full accountability. Though these are dark days for Silverport University, we are proactively working to improve our policies and ensure that Silverport provides a safe environment for students to learn and excel. We believe the accusations in no way reflect Silverport's policy and reputation for outstanding scholarship and research. Nevertheless, we will work hard to restore confidence in both the public and student body, whose trust we treasure."

For more information, please contact Katrina Norrins, Vice President, Public Relations for Student Affairs, 1-665-344-2524, or Katrina_Norrins@silverport.edu.
--
THIS IS A RUSH TRANSCRIPT. THIS COPY MAY NOT BE IN ITS FINAL FORM AND MAY BE UPDATED.

Silverport University Football Player Interview; Harry Anderson-Reese
LXB-TV Interview   11-15-2006

HARRY ANDERSON-REESE, LXB ANCHOR: We start this evening with an exclusive interview with Chet Buckley, one of the Silverport University football players facing accusations of impropriety in the Silverport University Sex Incentive Scandal.

Welcome, Chet.

CHET BUCKLEY, SILVERPORT UNIVERSITY FOOTBALL PLAYER: Thank you, Harry, for giving me the opportunity to give my side of the story.

ANDERSON-REESE: All right, what do you have to say about the allegations that honor students were recruited as hired escorts for Silverport's football team? Did the team receive sexual favors as an incentive to play better?

BUCKLEY: First, I would like to state that the accusations brought against the entire football team -- and our coach -- are completely groundless. We were not approached by any of the faculty, nor did we approach anyone asking for sexual favors of any sort. Yes, some of us were involved with some of the accusers, but it was consensual and in no case was any money involved...

ANDERSON-REESE: Are you saying that the accusations are false?

BUCKLEY: That is correct. There was nothing even remotely close to a "sex ring" thing going on. Everyone would go to parties at the campus pub and things would happen, you know, but not because the coach, or a prof, or a guidance counselor acted as a pimp or anything. That's just crazy. Those guys never do anything for students to begin with. Come on, coaches are always on your back *not* to do It before the big game! They're not gonna serve up some egghead for you...

ANDERSON-REESE: If these allegations are false, then why have several Silverport students come forward with these accusations?

BUCKLEY: I don't know why they're making those claims. They're just false. Maybe some of them want some attention and don't know how else to get it.

ANDERSON-REESE: Anything else you would like to add?

BUCKLEY: Yes, I just want to – to say again that the accusations are completely groundless. I would encourage people to visit my web site www.chetbuckleydefense.com to read and understand my side of the story – and to watch film clips of my previous games, to get a better understanding of what I'm really about and capable of.

ANDERSON-REESE: Thank you for your time.

BUCKLEY: No problem. Thanks for having me on your show.
--
Subject: Media Strategy
Date: 11/20/06
From: katrina_norrins@silverport.edu
To: travis_tanner@silverport.edu

Travis –

I understand the concerns over the handling of this matter you have outlined in your previous email. It's very disheartening that the media chooses to dwell on the sensational and – as of yet – unproven allegations, instead of focusing on Silverport's positive contributions to the community, such as our new Media Studies program. While I understand that the optics of this current situation may seem unsettling, am I certain the truth will prevail and

Silverport will be exonerated of these charges.

Please, be assured I am giving this matter my full, and undivided attention, and I am working with several students who can provide a counterbalance to these charges, and are willing to give media interviews on their positive experiences at Silverport University.

KN.

--

Kristi Bellows
A Chronicle about Living the Dream

November 29, 2006
Floating Over the Chilling Clouds of Darkness
Mood: Hopeful

Good news! Someone's finally has given me the chance to tell MY SIDE of the story. *Weekly Connect* (that's right, *that* national newsmagazine) ran a two-and-a-half page profile about me and my battle against Silverport University (which I have discussed here). I really liked how my pictures turned out in there. Pensive, sad, but determined to go on with my tattered little life – and still looking really hot and kick-ass in burgundy.

I can't believe that has been the only silver lining my dark cloud has offered me. I lost my scholarship, had to drop out of Silverport, change my address and phone number, and endure the rants of scum suckers from all over the world, including the reporter from that awful tabloid, who not only did not adequately address my side of this scandal, but somehow dug up unbelievably UNFLATTERING pictures of me! AND he MISSPELLED MY NAME! It's "Kristi," not "Kristy." Not only is not spelling my name right completely unprofessional, but it's going to fall through the virtual cracks of cyberspace if someone wants to do a database search about me (not to mention possibly give me a lower popularity rating on the major search engines).

Well, it doesn't matter, because there is actually a piece of good news: some indie director wants me to audition for a role in one of his movies. So, despite all this horror, I am finally going to get to live my dream. To all of those who've supported me, thank you for being there! *hugs* It means everything! Love you all! XOXO!!!
--

Silverport President Outlines Four-Point Plan; Hanna Shabat
AMERICAN DAILY INTELLIGENSER   12-09-2006

ORION, C.A. – Embattled Silverport University President Travis Tanner outlined late yesterday evening, his three-point plan to deal with his university's ever-worsening Sex Incentive Scandal.

In an email sent to faculty and students, Tanner did not address the nature of the allegations, but outlined his concerns, and plans to tackle the problem, which included:

- Improving student-faculty communications;
- Investigating claims of sexual impropriety instigated by university faculty;
- Creating student-faculty-community leader committees aimed at finding ways to improve student life on campus;
- Launching several initiatives aimed at encouraging students to report cases of sexual harassment.

Page 2...
--

Kristi Bellows
A Chronicle about Living the Dream

December 8, 2006
Shocked...
Mood: Furious

Victims of abuse just continue to be further abused by society. I
can't even breathe right now. I can honestly say that if it wasn't
for my therapist and this journal (and of course, all my fans,
XOXO), I would have already slashed my wrists a long time
ago.

As I mentioned here, I was up for an audition with an up-and-
coming indie director. I think it went well, but it's a bit part. I
was really proud of my acting! I just let my pain and despair
guide me into one boffo performance. I mean it, I kicked ass.

And then my world came crashing down. Chet Buckley – yes,
the one who had the helmet fetish – the man who just used me
and used me and then have the nerve to claim he did nothing
wrong – got a BOOK DEAL with a GHOST-WRITER (be-
cause Chet is just too illiterate to put two words together all by
himself) to tell his lies. I get the bit role in a small film – he gets a
book! And the guidance counselor, the one who got me involved
in this whole mess in the first place, was suspended WITH
FULL PAY! And he's going on all the network talk shows, deny-
ing he did anything wrong. And yesterday, on *News Breakers*, he
vowed he would write a book that would prove he was innocent.

The sexism in this society is just sick. Victims are just given little
scraps; the abusers are given the riches. It's not fair.
--
hOnEyNiNjA7: BOO!
KYJellyboy: hey u

hOnEyNiNjA7: Did you see me? Did you?

KYJellyboy: yeah, i saw u.

hOnEyNiNjA7: And?

KYJellyboy: u rocked

hOnEyNiNjA7: I was soooo nervous! Never did a talk show! I just wished it was more about me than Kristi.

KYJellyboy: it will b 1 day. How did ur audition go?

hOnEyNiNjA7: I made the last cut!!!!! Two more rounds to go! I'm so excited! I'm going to be on a TV show!

KYJellyboy: that show where u have 2 live with brainerz n jocks until 1 of u is left?

hOnEyNiNjA7: That's the one!

KYJellyboy: i guess u can thank Kristi 4 that 1...heheheheh...

hOnEyNiNjA7: Never! She's a bitch! If my parents found out about my part, they'd slay me with an axe! She should have kept her big mouth shut!

KYJellyboy: bummer

hOnEyNiNjA7: I'm just trying to make the best out of a bad situation.

KYJellyboy: whatever rox ur world babe & btw, saw ur new up-loaded movie on starmaker.com. can't believe u got all those hits!

hOnEyNiNjA7: Thanks! At least there are people who are interested in hearing the truth about me out there. Have to go now, hon. I still have to study for my finals. Bye!

--

Subject: Re: Basil Emery

Date: 12/14/06

From: katrina_norrins@silverport.edu

To: travis_tanner@silverport.edu

Travis –

We are working overtime on this urgent matter. The entire department is in crisis mode. We regret that we did not foresee

Professor Emery's late-night confession to the police that he was an active participant in securing paid student escorts for the football team, in exchange for a percentage of the profits. However, his confession has not yet been corroborated, and it does not necessarily reflect upon the integrity of this institution. We are actively working one-on-one with the press; and we are setting up several interviews and a press conference to deal with the matter.

I am confident that we will survive this current crisis while preserving Silverport's stellar reputation.

KN.

--

Previous page…

CONTINUED: **WORLD EXCLUSIVE: Silverport University Professor's Tawdry Tale of Sex and Greed "I was Professor Pimp!"**
Bill Scheck's Siren Screams
LONDON WORLD BULLETIN   12-22-2006

But I can now reveal that Professor Pimp's repulsive ways are being handsomely rewarded: Hollywood is calling!

Fire Breather Studios have optioned Emery's torrid story and plan to release a major motion picture of his sexcapades as early as next summer. Rumors swirl that leading Hollywood heartthrob and Oscar winner Nigel Cox will play mastermind Emery in the film.

--

Subject: Announcement
Date: 12/24/06
From: mari_white@silverport.edu
To: staff@silverport.edu

It is with great sadness that we announce that Katrina Norrins will be leaving the College and her position as Vice President, Public Relations for Student Affairs effective immediately. Katrina has decided to leave her position to spend more time with her family. We wish Katrina the best.

Mari White
Assistant to the President

The Exclusive

I

"… calling it a slap in the face to victims of violence everywhere." Reporting live from the Steel City courthouse, this is Bradley Cross, WSC-TV News."

The camera stopped rolling. The Serious Journalist face and alto voice could disappear and Brad finally could crack a playful smirk at the cameraman. He then turned around and looked up at the majestic courthouse roof and the bleary, opaque sky. Usually, Brad looked better and healthier under sunnier conditions. No matter. His voice still sounded commanding enough to make up for any deficiencies in Nature's late-autumn lighting.

Besides, the story was powerful enough, and that was saying something, given people's penchant for rampant media promiscuity in the modern age. Exclusive interviews with newsmaker subjects hardly existed at all anymore: most people not only would give as many interviews as journalists' wanted, but they would shill themselves continually on their own little websites and blogs. Everyone was everywhere: it seemed as if no one was special anymore.

Elusive sources and scoops still remained to be hunted down and displayed over the airwaves, but finding them became more dif-

ficult, as was presenting them in just the right way to the audience: people would clam up when they knew their dirty deeds
were becoming public knowledge. The lawyers, public relations
hacks, and image consultants certainly made certain of that.
There was always an army of manure shovelers cleaning up the
messes the troublemaker would leave behind. People were tightlipped about their secrets. Idealism in the masses was a thing of
the past, and everyone would only give you meaningful face-
time, if they could get something out of it. No one admitted
wrongdoing; they would just blame the media for refusing to go
along with the charade.

Even if the coveted troublemaker did concede to sit in the hot
seat, subjects these days were too media-savvy to be trapped into
a boffo confession: they still would try to spin and justify their
own odious actions in front of rolling cameras. No one was
wrong, evil, greedy, selfish, criminal, psychopathic, or dangerous. They were misunderstood, and persecuted for being different. Everyone was a victim of the press. Even the audience believed that and would complain about a journalist's tough line of
questioning. The guilty were to be pitied for getting caught.

Brad took a cigarette and lighter from his jacket pocket. Yes, his
story was good. Very good. Better than average, at least. It
would get him some attention; after all, it was the second story of
the newscast. It wasn't the lead story, unfortunately, but for a
TV reporter who had been in the business for less than two
years; it was a step in the right direction. If only he could break
the right barrier, he could make the right waves and get a better
job in a bigger market. But the right opportunity had not presented itself in Steel City just yet.

Brad did not want to wait forever: he wanted a more prominent
position within the year. How would he get enough people to
pay attention to him and tune in just to see him shine? Where

was the elusive scoop that would put him on the map, once and for all?

The competition amongst reporters in this city was sadistic and unrelenting. The newspaper reporters were particularly aggressive and vile, when in pursuit of a story. The scribes at the *Vigilance* were deluded into believing they were the sole Chosen Messengers; so they were always out for blood against anyone outside their newsroom. And some reporters were more treacherous to compete with than others. Maggie Lyme was the worst offender. She had been a journalist for barely a year-and-a-half and she already made an enviable name for herself with her outrageously devious and dubious tactics. Lyme had the reputation of being a scheming and scamming party girl, who could find the scoop before anyone else knew there was a scoop to be found. How could Brad compete with the feral and intrepid Ms Lyme, whose wily hunting instincts had proven to be preternaturally unerring?

Fortunately, Brad had no intention of getting ahead playing by the same rule book as Lyme. No network evening news anchor could afford to take the risks she did. It was all right to be reporting in a war zone: so long as the hair looked tended and the shirt was clean. He could not get down and dirty to find explosive information. Lyme wasn't afraid to crawl through a booby-trapped, snake-infested sewer to get the story, but then again, she didn't have to worry about looking crisp and professional in front of a camera once she came out. The trick was to find the right kind of scoop: one that would get attention and would matter to the nice viewers at home, but not the kind of story that would bring him in direct competition with Lyme. If her interest was aroused, she would best him. Worse, she would openly gloat over his loss in her story. He could not afford to be seen as weak or foolish.

The miserable sky showed no signs of softening its recalcitrant melancholy. It would rain in a matter of minutes; no doubt about it. All the signs were there: the damp smell, the swelling clouds, the darkening sky; the restless birds in flight. As Brad began to think about his predicament, the cameraman interrupted his thoughts.

"Hope it clears up by tonight."

"Not a chance."

"They didn't call for rain. You never know…"

"I know. It's going to be thunderstorm for certain. Any minute now."

"Damn, I was hoping to…"

"Make other plans, Mike. Take my word for it, or just look around you. It's going to be one nasty storm."

What a stupid Pollyanna moron, thought Brad as he began to briskly walk from the courthouse entrance to the WSC van. That's why Mike was a mere cameraman. It didn't take any effort to point and shoot. It was mindless work for a mindless drone. *They didn't call for rain…* You never know! Relying on the words of others, instead of looking for signs was a recipe for disaster. Heaven save us from the Mikes of the world.

Getting into the passenger seat, Brad threw away his half-smoked cigarette on the asphalt and slammed the door shut. Within seconds, the first drops of rain began to fall, before the downpour came and drenched Mike as he tried to quickly put the equipment into the van, close the back door and jump into the driver's seat. Brad merely glanced at his watch, then quickly looked away.

II

How anyone could stand to work at WSC-TV was a mystery, Brad wondered, looking at his computer screen and starting to read the morning wire-stories at his desk. The computers were fairly new and the chairs serviceable enough, but still, everything else in the newsroom hinted at a grand institution that was in decline. The size of the newsroom was obviously made to hold many more bodies – the number of people present now was far less than it was decades before. The group pictures of the WSC staff over the years, had dwindled from majestic to pathetic. Management was squeezing every dime they could: the easiest ones to squeeze were the employees.

Then, there were management's fanatically Spartan sensibilities: the number of investigative pieces decreased, as the number of cheaper, fluffy wire-stories increased. Every penny that could be squeezed out of the newsroom was squeezed with precision. Cell phone use was counted by the half penny, and even photocopying was frowned upon, unless absolutely necessary. No matter: Brad wanted out. No decent journalist deserved to be forced to work in a place that made you count the number of paper clips you were using, instead of the number of leads you were chasing. If WSC didn't appreciate his brilliance, and winsome looks, then some other larger market station would. The only thing standing in his way was his lack of significant scoops.

Seeing nothing significant on the wire to help him achieve his professional ambitions, Brad began calling up some of his trusted contacts for possible leads, although, that also seemed to be an exercise in futility: no quirky, steamy court cases, no outrage-inducing cookies, not even the slightest hint of anything illegal that would grab the upper middle class's undivided attention. There was one reported fatality: a shooting in Steel City's lower east end. However, that part of town was notorious for its rampant lower-class crime, and vile street gangs such as the Death

Squads and the Hatchet Kings. The murder was most likely just another byproduct of that part of the city's violent way of life.

Brad's cell phone rang. "Bradley Cross here."

"Cross, I got something for you I think you'd be interested in." It was one of Cross's less important police sources who occasionally provided him with inside information for some of his violent crime stories. It was usually Brad who called him. Enduring the cop's monotone voice and minor tidbits wasn't a pleasure, but at least the man was reliable, if boring.

"What's up?"

"You know that murder this morning in the lower east end?"

"Heard about it," Brad sighed somewhat curtly. This call would be a waste of time. "What's special about it?"

"It turned out to be a botched carjacking. At least, it looks that way," said the police officer, but with an uncharacteristic hint of excitement in his usually drab and droning voice.

"What's so special about *this* carjacking?" Brad asked more animatedly, sensing that there may be an element of intrigue.

"It's the victim…"

"I'm listening."

"It's Sharon Welles – the pregnant wife of that loaded advertising guru Grant Welles."

"Grant Welles' wife? What was she doing there?"

"Who knows? Maybe she got lost. She was found near her car with a gunshot wound to the head. This is big news."

Finally, Bradley Cross had the break he desperately needed.

III

The lead proved to be a fruitful one: the gentle, comely Sharon Welles was a beloved figure in the normally jaded Steel City and her unexpected and mysterious slaying was an instant super-story and audience magnet. Who killed Sharon? What was the motive? Why would the lapinesque beauty dare to venture any-where near the city's east end? What would Grant Welles do to avenge the deaths of his beloved wife and unborn baby?

The last question was particularly important to Steel City citi-zens: Welles was known as a reclusive, no-nonsense businessman who, when he did make the occasional public statement, spoke movingly of his late wife. Though Welles made his fortune in the advertising business, he himself shunned the media spotlight al-most entirely.

However, today would be an exception: Welles had agreed to speak at a police news conference. Since Sharon's body was dis-covered, there had been little evidence to indicate who the killer or what the motive was. What was known was that Sharon was supposed to drive herself to her obstetrician for a regularly scheduled appointment. When she did not arrive, the office called her husband, who was at their home conducting a busi-ness meeting with an out-of-town client. Fearing for his six-month pregnant wife, Welles called the police. The Welles' maid confirmed that her employer had been at home at the time of alleged car-jacking. When Sharon's body was found, her hus-band could not provide any insight, as to why his wife strayed so far away from her regular route.

Brad considered the public facts of the case at the press confer-ence as he watched a pained and fragmented Welles tearfully plead to the public to come forward with any information they may have about the senseless and brutal crime that denied him of his family. The emotions of the widower were raw and powerful, and made for compelling television. Brad covered the press conference and felt that his comments and commentary helped shape the story. There was only one obstacle that had given him some feelings of anxiety.

Maggie Lyme was covering the Welles case for the *Steel City Vigilance.*

There she stood, in the back corner of the room, whispering and flirting with a young, attractive police officer who not only seemed to relish the libidinous journalist's shameless overtures, but was returning the sly looks and raw, if muted body signals. Maggie wasn't paying attention to Welles' pained pleas for help: she was too busy paying attention to her attractive playmate and her baser desires. Brad watched in disgust as he kept a close eye on the conference. Eavesdropping on her conversation would take some clandestine effort.

"What do you say, Foley?" Maggie asked the young police officer as she seductively fixed the young man's tie.

"You're on!" the eager policeman replied and moved closer to the object of his lust. Neither looked even remotely interested at the weeping man who begged the public to help him find his wife and unborn son's murderer. But then again, good-looking men were always Maggie's weak spot. She wasn't paying attention and was too busy making a date with the studly young officer to notice the breaking news around her. The attractive rookie was around the same age as she, with short, black hair, gleaming blue eyes, and a dimpled, infectious smile. Maggie always gravitated toward the handsomest man in the room. At least she was consistent.

Could Brad take advantage of his rival's hormones to out- scoop her and the rest of the reporters in Steel City?

It was a risky plan; after all, one could really never tell if Lyme really was paying attention or not. But if she wasn't, and if he could play his cards right, then perhaps he would find the leverage he so desperately needed to get out the Steel City newsroom. Getting one up on Maggie Lyme would be a bonus: it would show him to be superior to the city's most promising young journalist. Her professional upset would simply help enhance his image.

Welles' press conference was a great visual, but so far, the man himself refused to grant any media interviews, lest it hurt the murder investigation. Welles had said as much: he did not want to turn his tragedy into a media circus that would distract the police from hunting down the guilty party. That made sense, but what if Brad could get the grieving widower to give him an exclusive interview? It would be tricky: Welles was a notorious recluse who did not want to be in the spotlight. Yet, what if Brad could convince him he would cover the story tastefully and poignantly so that Welles' word would help the investigation instead of hinder it?

There was too much at stake for him not to give it a try: Welles' emotional cry complemented his pithy, profound sound bites and compelling story. The fascinating man was a well-known commodity in the city and had the goodwill of its citizens. The mystery was grisly and, as yet, unsolved. Sharon was a pregnant and gorgeous woman who wandered in the seedy part of town. If Brad could only get Welles to speak to him and only him…

It would be a pure ratings cleanup.

IV

The hunt for Grant Welles turned out to be more difficult than Brad had envisioned. Calls left to Welles' business offices had been left unanswered – not just for Brad, but for every journalist tracking down the elusive multimillionaire. Welles was hiding somewhere in seclusion; so he could not be approached in person. Finding his unlisted number had been harder than expected as well, but Brad called up a favor and managed to snag it. Unfortunately, he could only leave messages imploring Welles to speak to him, as part of the hunt to track down his wife's killer. This begging had gone on for two weeks. In desperation, Brad had tracked down various close employees of Welles to plea his case to their melancholy boss. Some rebuffed his requests, while a few relented and agreed to play pitchman on his behalf. The question was whether Welles would finally agree to an interview.

Sleep was out of the question: Brad had offices and a mansion to case in the hunt for employees to cajole. He interviewed family friends in an effort to learn more about Welles' habits, routines, and movements. He even looked through nearby dumpsters and trash cans for valuable leads. So far, his efforts had been wasted ones.

As he sat at his desk, the phone rang. He nervously picked up the receiver, trying to maintain his even-sounding voice. "Bradley Cross here."

"Mr. Cross," a female voice on the other end replied. "This is Sheryl Lansky, Grant Welles' personal assistant. This is in regard to your request for a television interview about his wife and son."

Brad's stomach felt heavy and unsettled. "Yes?"

"He usually doesn't grant media interviews, but after reviewing your request, he has agreed to talk to you about the case. With certain conditions, of course."

This is how Maggie Lyme must usually feel, Brad thought as he tried his best to sound serious and empathetic, rather than reveal his true, euphoric feelings.

V

The exclusive interview with Grant Welles was more than merely an enviable coup: it was his ladder to better things. Everyone had been talking about Brad's scoop for the last three days – from the producers in the newsroom to the posters in the chatrooms. It wasn't just everyone in the city who talked about Bradley Cross's finest moment as a reporter; his interview aired on other affiliate stations across the country. His name was everywhere: from the national newspapers to the network news. Of course, Grant Welles got top billing and rightfully so; but this was the biggest story in his career and now, thanks to a little ingenuity, Brad got more free quality media exposure than he could ever have hoped for.

The interview itself was rather short: Welles agreed to speak for no longer than twenty minutes. That condition alone put pressure on Brad to utilize his precious time as best as he could. The good news was that Welles was a mesmerizing guest who had much to offer during the interview. He revealed that one eyewitness had spotted several members of the Death Squads or Hatchet Kings roaming the area where Sharon's car was eventually found. Welles also discussed his relationship with his wife and how the killings tore into his spirit and soul.

While details about the case were lacking, Welles had given Brad so much color and raw emotion during the interview that the executive producer of the Six O'clock News Hour decided to run nearly the entire twenty minutes unedited. This gave Brad more than enough face time and exposure. But, the exclusive would be only the beginning: other survivors and victims of crime considered Brad to be the go-to reporter to discuss their personal travails, giving him a niche, and a steady stream of stories and airtime.

Best of all, Maggie Lyme had not managed to snag a single exclusive interview or lead since Brad's interview. This gave him great satisfaction: because she did not manage to outdo him or provide new fodder about the as yet unsolved murder, his exclusive gave him more mileage than usual. Everything was falling nicely into place.

As Brad finished getting dressed, his thoughts were abruptly interrupted by a loud, impudent knock on the door. He checked his watch: it was 6:31 am. Who would be visiting at this early hour? How did he or she manage to get past security? Was it a neighbor who needed help? He wondered about the unusual visitor as he opened his condo door and stared.

It was Maggie Lyme.

VI

Some rivals were more intimidating inside the arena than they were outside of it; they may be full of bravura and cunning during the match, but when the bout was done, their ordinary selves took over and they became just another unremarkable person. On the other hand, Maggie's presence outside her usual milieu almost seemed more terrifying than when she was in her element. She was wily and street smart; her sweet, charming, and disarming ways were usually her weapons of choice. Off hours, her smug, cocky demeanor was always unnerving; that was the way she psyched out rivals and sources alike to remind them at the end of the day, who was the predator and who was the prey. She always seemed to be in the know; always seemed to be sizing up her quarry. Though she was a soft, attractive woman, her long, fiery red hair, swagger and arrogant smirk were intimidating reminders of the hunter within.

But Brad kept his composure as he spoke. "Magnus D. Lyme," he declared slowly, studying his unexpected guest. "What are you doing here?"

"I came to congratulate you on your lovely little coup." She looked at him carefully.

"It was a *big* coup," Brad corrected her somewhat haughtily and continued to look at his colleague. Maggie straightened her posture even more, and then flashed a sweet, toothy grin. Brad seemed unmoved as he spoke. "But, seriously, why are you coming to see me this early?"

"I told you already: I came over to congratulate you. You should be proud of yourself. Everyone's still talking about your interview. I would have come over or called to give you my congrats a lot sooner, but things came up and … why am I telling you this? You're in the business."

"Is that the only reason you came over to see me?"

"Of course not," Maggie purred as she looked at him seductively. "Let me treat you to a nice little victory breakfast -- my treat, of course. You haven't had your breakfast yet, I hope."

"No, I haven't, but look; I really have to get to work..."

"Come on, Cross; don't be such a big baby," Maggie protested with an air of sultry confidence and playfulness, "I want to treat you, Braddie. Come on."

"Why do want to treat me?"

"It's the least I can do for the reporter of the hour."

Brad considered. He wanted to know what Maggie wanted from him, anyway; besides, it would give him the chance to gloat. She may have been putting on a brave face, but her ego had to be bruised. "All right, coffee and muffin. I don't have much time."

"Good. Let's go. We both have jobs to get to, and the sooner we go the better."

They walked across the street to a small, local diner that had the distinct reputation of serving cold, mediocre offerings twenty-four hours a day while playing old, mediocre music. But, for the moment, it would serve its purpose: a coffee and oatmeal muffin for Brad; a coffee and chocolate chip muffin for Maggie. Brad expected Maggie to make catty, biting putdowns over his victory, or at least try to pump him for information. He could not make heads or tails of her inner workings. She simply finished her meal and asked the waitress for the bill.

"You know, Cross," she finally spoke as she looked at the receipt, "I got to hand it to you: you certainly got the ambition and the ingenuity to get a rich guy like Welles to give a private performance of Act Three of his little play for you in your own little theater." She suddenly seemed too giddy as she spoke. Maggie Lyme never congratulated her rivals, and this speech was obviously no congratulations. At heart, she was perpetually cocky, but suddenly, her innate arrogance seemed nearly out of control: she was suppressing some bloodthirsty thrill and her smirk and the feral glee in her eyes said as much to Brad. "The interview was colorful enough and had a real emotional pull to it. Just like most of that press conference. Not a lot of new details about the case, though."

"He did say that an eyewitness saw the Death Squads or Hatchet Kings nearby."

"It's kind of strange that someone from that part of town couldn't tell the difference between the Squads and the Axes. Who found the witness, anyway? The cops didn't confirm it, did they?"

"Welles hired a private investigator. I'm sure he's the one who tracked that one down."

"Did you actually confirm that with the investigator personally...?" Before she could say anything else, a slightly annoyed Brad cut in.

"Still sore that I out scooped you with the Welles' interview, eh Maggie?"

"Sore? I am absolutely thrilled that you nailed that interview. Really, Cross. I couldn't be happier."

"Cut the crap and the theatrics, Maggie. I bested you, you hate being bested and we both know it. If you hadn't been so busy trying to snag a date with that leering rookie at the Welles' press conference, maybe you would have…"

"Whoa, whoa, Cross, back up there. What 'date' are you talking about?" Maggie asked sharply. She raised an eyebrow and took out her wallet to pay for their meal. She looked genuinely perplexed.

"I overheard you when you asked him out. You said, and I quote, 'What do you say, Foley,' and he said, 'You're on.' What do you call that? I heard it and took advantage of it."

Maggie's eyes widened and she began to laugh.

"That wasn't me making a date, you eavesdropping dummy. I was making a friendly little bet with him."

"About what?" Brad asked. He began to feel uneasy.

"Oh, nothing really important – it was just an innocent little wager between friends about some minor detail of the case."

"Who won?"

"I did, of course." Maggie placed the money and the bill on the table, and got up. "That's the cash that paid for our breakfast. Anyway, I have to go now. I had a long night and I have even a longer day ahead of me. Catch you later, Cross."

With one final grin, she quickly left the table.

Brad had to control himself to keep from fainting or screaming. He knew that Maggie's smile was no random act or a show of pleasantry! She was up to something devious and the breakfast was all part of her cunning game. She came to his condo at an extremely early hour – why would she do that unless there was a reason? But what could it be?

Then, at once, Brad knew: the news -- she didn't want him to read the newspaper, listen or watch the morning reports. Something must have happened in the Welles case. But what happened during the time Maggie never once asked any details of his exclusive?

He ran from the restaurant and to the nearest *Vigilance* vending box, grabbed some change from his pocket and bought a copy of the morning's paper. As he read the front page of the *Steel City Vigilance*, he screamed in agony.

VII
EXCLUSIVE: Welles Confesses to Police: 'I killed my pregnant wife myself'

Wealthy businessman's tale of carjacking a hoax

By Magnus D. Lyme, Staff Reporter

Steel City – In a shocking twist to the brutal mystery that has gripped the city, advertising entrepreneur Grant Welles has confessed to the murder of his six month pregnant wife Sharon, who was allegedly shot to death during a botched hijacking in the city's lower east end. Welles has been charged with first degree murder and is being held at the Steel City Regional jail.

Welles, 38, turned himself in to the police late last night, and admitted to shooting his 36-year-old wife in the head last month. Steel City Police confirmed that Welles is being held in connection with the murder and that he surrendered voluntarily. According to one law enforcement official, an emotionally distraught Welles told police, "I killed my pregnant wife myself. I can't take that haunting midnight voice anymore." Police confirm that Welles surrendered at the downtown police station Thursday night. He was not accompanied by his lawyer, J. Crane Harding. He also confessed to have secretly rented a lower east side apartment, where he kept the gun he used to kill his wife.

On November 25, Sharon Welles had reportedly left the upper west end mansion that she shared with her husband to go to her scheduled doctor's appointment. When she did not return home, Welles called the police to report his wife missing.

Neighbors expressed shock over the slaying, but maintained throughout the investigation, that relations between Welles and his wife of seven years had been idyllic. They all described Sharon as a delicate, sensitive woman who volunteered at an animal shelter and a children's cancer center, and Welles as a doting, caring husband.

The murder sent shock waves through the city, since initial reports had suggested that the town's most notorious street gangs, the Death Squads or Hatchet Kings, may have been responsible for Sharon's death.

However, suspicion never fell on Welles, since the well-known businessman had a seemingly airtight alibi: both his housekeeper and an out-of-town client claimed they both were with Welles at the time of Sharon's murder. According to one police source who asked not to be named, Welles admitted that he tricked his associate and the maid into giving him an alibi by turning several of his clocks back 50 minutes, giving the illusion that he had been with them during that critical time period.

Earlier reports also suggested Sharon was killed because she had accidentally gotten off the wrong ramp and had found herself in the city's most dangerous neighborhood. Police now say Welles convinced his wife to go to the area, by falsely claiming that the animal shelter where she volunteered had asked her to pick up a litter of stray cats.

Brad Cross, one of WSC-TV's investigative reporters, was given an "exclusive" interview by Welles earlier this week. In that interview, Welles claimed that "psychopathic drug dealers" may have been responsible for murdering his wife.

"Everyone who has come to support me at this horrible time has my undying gratitude. For one afternoon, I thought my wife and unborn baby would be safe during a simple trip to the doctor's office. Had I known what terrifying, brutal fate awaited them both at the hands of banded drug dealers and killers, I would have gone with her and sacrificed myself for my wife and son," Welles told Cross at the time, though it appears that interview was an attempt to cover up his own role in his wife's murder.

Tensions between police and city's black community came to a head earlier in the investigation, when Welles claimed one eyewitness allegedly saw a "band of menacing-looking black men" in the area where Sharon's car was later discovered.

See "Welles' hoax," page A3.

The Godblaze Curiosity

I

A wasted trip.
A wasted trip.
A wasted trip.
A wasted trip.

No scrap today.
No finds today.
No deals today.
No cash today.

No food tonight.

An empty town.
A lonely town.
A hopeless town.
A dead-end town.

No jobs here.
No exits here.
No plans here.
No foundation here.

No dreams here.

Nothing.
Nothing.
Nothing.
Nothing.

We are animals here.
We are poor here.
We are scared here.
We are wild here.

We are nearly dead here.

Must go out tomorrow.
Must go forward tomorrow.
Must go searching tomorrow.
Must go on tomorrow.

Go.
Survive.
Push.
Hunt.

Amen.

II

Just one white glint would make the day a profitable one: one tiny flash and the week's worries would be put to sleep. Metal was as good as gold in these parts, and finding the right bits would put more than just scraps on the dinner table. It wasn't much to ask for – it was the most basic of requests: please, don't let us make it through another day without food.

It was a humiliating request considering that not everyone in the area was so destitute. In fact, the coastal city itself certainly had its share of beauty and prosperity: the land was lush enough to make agricultural pursuits worthwhile, and there was enough work for skilled workers to keep busy. For the farmers and the tradesmen life was bearable. Not extravagant, just bearable. The shopkeepers could manage without outside help, relying instead on themselves, or their wives and children to do the daily chores. It wasn't a glorious life with endless possibilities, but at least the shopkeepers, tradesmen, and farmers found hope and solace in prayer. For the highly educated, it was a grand life with endless perks. The university groomed the well-heeled, in order for them to prosper in the high-rises upon graduation and unwind on the beaches after hours.

For the uneducated and unskilled living on the fringes, it was a matter of mere survival. For them, this was a nameless dead-end town with nameless citizens – not a city, of hope or limitless potential. There was no reason for the well-heeled to make any tracks here – there wasn't enough of anything to exploit.

Without the rich or ambitious, there were the consequences. Factories closed. Businesses folded. Even the local hospital had to shut down three years ago. Restaurants were scarce and a social life was nearly out of the question. There was nothing much to talk about other than local gossip or old news from far away: some people in town still prattled about the old Nazi who killed himself in Spandau, or about some hearings concerning a Colonel shredding some documents with a pretty blonde secretary, but those were scratches of old news that seemed to a have a longer shelf life here than anywhere else. Whatever the news, people in these parts didn't always keep current. There were other, more immediate pressures to worry about.

The outside world wasn't all that important to the farmers or shopkeepers, and scavengers and squatters living in the margins didn't have the time or energy to ponder about anything out of city limits. What was important was finding the next meal, but finding the meal depended on getting enough scrap to sell. Right now, at this dark and early hour, the white glint was all that mattered, the spry young man thought as his shorter, stouter partner and he stood in front of the ruins of an abandoned building that once served as some sort of specialized hospital. Yesterday, the abandoned factory building had proved useless. Today, something had to have the white glint. Or else they would have to go home with an empty wheel-barrow again.

No, that wouldn't be the case: there had to be something within that crumbling debris. There had to be something worthwhile to find there…unless, of course, the scavengers who came before them did manage to pick it clean over the last three years. No choice and no chance to ponder the odds; the young man's companion began to climb the debris and dig for metal. All they had between them were a hammer, pick, flashlight, and a wheelbarrow.

Fortunately, the building hadn't entirely caved in: there were enough preserved rooms and corridors to almost guarantee that the semi-intact rooms promised those brave enough to enter unknown and worthwhile treasure. The holes were large enough to enter without problems. No guards around. The task looked simple enough. Almost. The thought of digging, finding, reaping, and the cashing in was a good enough reason to venture inside.

The taller of the two young men whistled to his companion who slowly turned around and shrugged as he asked, "What?"

"Let's go in. Something has to be there."

"You sure?"

"Got another idea?"

"Not really."

"Move it then."

"What do you think is in there? Iron? Lead?"

"Don't know 'til we get {in} there. Probably both. Let's go."

III

The meandering and laborious trek to the basement proved to be a tricky one: between the inconvenient darkness, uncooperative squatters living within the squalid ruins, and the treacherous debris, groping proved dangerous at best. It was still too early for the sunlight to provide the scavengers any sense of certainty and their flashlight was of little use so far. The dampness did nothing to help matters. To top off their misery, there was little to show for their persistence, yet the horror of failure forced the two adventurers to press on.

As the first patches of illuminating haze broke through the dark sky, the scavengers were still struggling to find their way around the junk in the ruins. True to their recent luck, the newly glistening sunlight would be of no benefit to them, the skinnier of the scavengers grumbled to himself as he looked around with the care and intensity of an archeologist on a groundbreaking dig. It was too dark to determine whether the scraps left behind were of any value – there was no point in endangering themselves by pulling things out of the wreckage and carrying the heavy loads back to the top, if they could not get a decent fee – or worse, not get a fee at all. Everything was a judgment call and nothing was going well.

"I found something," the young man's partner barked so loud that he startled his normally languid friend. He turned around to see what was the cause of the sudden excitement. Taking the flashlight, he turned the flickering beam toward his partner and the object in question.

It was something substantial, all right, and if they could get it out, could be extremely profitable. But, the logistics didn't look good.

"What do you think it is? Some kind of machine?"

"Hospital equipment. Big. Lots of metal in it. Something fancier than an X-ray machine. Don't know what, though. Never go to the doctor when I'm sick."

"What do you think?"

"Must be worth money. Let's take it."

"We can't put the whole thing into the wheelbarrow. Come on!"

"I know that, dummy. We'll take it apart here."

"How? We never took something like that apart before."

"Anyway we can. Shut up and let's get to work. I don't want to stand in the dark, hang around with you all day."

"What if it blows up or something?"

"It won't. Probably doesn't work anymore, anyway. Why else would they leave it here? Let's move it."

Using their hammer and pick, the two men began to take the machine apart. It was a slow job that seemed increasingly futile with each thrust and pull: the machine proved sturdy, even as it lay buried in the rubble, even with the neglect caused by its long abandonment in a dank, foul basement. Yet, the two scavengers refused to concede until they took the machine apart, and found themselves staring at the metallic innards of their dismantled prize. Looking inside they saw their treasure chest: a large lead canister still nesting in its original position.

"What is it?"

"Dunno."

"What do we do with it?"

"We take it. Gotta be worth something if it was that hard to get to it."

"What's inside that thing?"

"Dunno. Let's take it out and put it in the wheelbarrow. We'll take it apart somewhere else."

IV

So little to show for so much work, thought the scavenger leader as he sat on the dusty ground and stared angrily at his leaden adversary. The canister was supposed to be their treasure chest, but right now, that desperate fantasy was on life support. Taking the lead canister apart proved to be strenuous and painful work – with no latch or lock, the job was a thankless, grueling task. Whatever goodness resided inside was stubbornly trying to remain a closely-guarded secret.

But the determined man would not give up without a fight. The lid of the canister finally gave way when the scavenger began to vigorously pull apart the pieces. As the top of the canister fell to the ground, he felt a painful burning sensation sear his hands and arms.

"Ow! Man, dammit!" the young man yelped and he dropped both parts of the canister to the ground.

"What happened?"

"Damn thing's burned my hands."

"Really?"

"What did I just say?"

"What kind of lead burns your hands?" the stouter of the two asked. He took the canister off the ground and emptied the contents. A tiny capsule with a small window fell to the ground and the man winced, as his partner did seconds before. He dropped the casing and shook his hands.

"What is this crazy stuff? Burned me, too."

"Something weird and probably worth something big."

The two partners looked down at the metal box within the metal box. It was small a lead capsule. Both went down on their knees to take a closer look. It was the small window that got their attention: what greeted their gazes was a gentle blue light, shimmering peacefully inside. The radiant beauty was hypnotic and calming.

Instinctively, each man considered his options as he admired the peaceful flickers: the blue light must be valuable: it was housed in an iron canister and capsule. The container alone could fetch something at the local iron shop. But the light itself … its beauty must be worth a small fortune.

The shorter of the two scavengers gingerly picked up the capsule and threw it in the wheelbarrow. "What the hell is it? Can't figure it out. A gem of some sort?" he asked his partner, looking at the fresh, raw burns on his hands and arms.

"Never seen one shine like that," the lankier of the two noted and shook his head. He considered what else it could be, but couldn't provide his partner with a satisfactory answer. "Hospitals don't keep stuff like diamonds and sapphires. But it's gotta be something special since it glows like that years after the place closed up."

"Yeah, has to be something huge. And expensive."

"But I can't take this apart. We'll have to sell it like this. Let them do the dirty work."

The man picked up the capsule from the wheelbarrow to study it once more. The light. Its rich cobalt hue sang as it shone in its metallic prison. He placed it carefully back into the wheelbarrow. The men looked at each other and nodded. It was time to take a quick trip to the junkyard.

Unlike their morning dig, the afternoon trek proved to be an uneventful one. Once they reached their destination, it would be a matter of explaining the worth of an object that neither man could fully understand, but knew would be a rare and exciting item that few people could resist. The junkyard owner and his wife had agreed to see the young men and had stood at the entrance. Beside them was the owner's brother, who was somewhat younger than his middle-aged sibling, and did nothing to hide his curiosity from the visitors; in fact, he looked almost giddy in contrast to his stern-looking brother and sister-in-law.

"What you got?" the owner finally asked curtly as he rubbed his nose and sniffed at nothing in particular.

It was the taller scavenger who answered, "Some iron case with some shiny stuff inside. Found it at the old hospital this morning. Look here." The young man picked up the capsule and showed it to the junkyard owner.

The owner and his brother both leaned forward to have a better look at the blue light silently humming its peaceful song in the little window.

"Is that a diamond in there?" the owner finally asked coldly.

"Don't think so. Something better. Something shinier than a diamond, anyway."

"Shinier than a diamond?" The junkyard owner's brother seemed impressed as his eyes widened and his voice bellowed. What was this wonderful and magical substance that was so special that it had to be encased iron and {be} hidden in the bowels

259

of the old hospital?

The scrap metal man stared at the capsule, trying hard not to reveal his excitement over this extraordinary discovery. Usually, these two scavengers weren't known for their competency or quality of finds. This capsule was an accidental find, the owner was certain, and he knew neither man would know what the substance was, nor how much to ask for it. He didn't know what the strange blue substance was either, but at least he knew how to barter on the fly, and at that moment, that was the only thing that counted.

"Don't know what I'd do with it…" he began.

"You found it at the hospital? Did it cure the sick?" interrupted his brother.

"Guess it did. Found it in a machine," one of the scavengers replied and shrugged.

"Doesn't mean much to me," the owner interjected, trying to maintain control over the bargaining.

"But, look at that light. Bet you never saw anything like that anywhere. And they hid it in the hospital. It's got to be something," countered the taller of the two guests.

If the owner was at least trying to gain control with a poker face, his brother made no attempt to hide his excitement about the uncanny find. Something so exotic must have been sent to the town by God Himself. Yes, it was the only logical explanation possible.

"What do you think it is? Fire from the gods?" the brother asked reverently as he pushed toward the scavengers and touched the capsule with his hands.

The shrewder of the two considered. If the mere novelty of the light wouldn't jack up the price, then appealing to the religious angle would always do the trick in these parts. The owner's brother would not be able to resist, even if his brother could. A sale was a sale, besides, there were three things that could always turn a dollar in a dead-end place like this: sex, scams, and religion. It was time to use the latter two on the scavenger's mark.

"Could be." The lanky scavenger nodded. "We did find it in a hospital. Could be for good luck, or it could have been used to cure people. That's probably why they hid it and didn't tell nobody about it. They'd want people to think it was them who made sickness go away, not the angels."

"What do they call it?" the brother asked.

"Godblaze," the scavenger blurted in a moment of inspiration, "I think they call it Godblaze."

"Godblaze?" gasped the brother as he grabbed the capsule and fingered it nervously. "That's what it's called?"

"I never heard about a 'Godblaze...'" began the junkyard owner angrily.

"It's called whatever the good man wants it called. Obviously, it's a good luck thing. So, how much for it?"

"If it's so lucky, why do you want to sell it?" the wife finally asked as she suspiciously looked at her two guests.

"Hey, if *you* buy it, *we* consider ourselves very lucky. Well?"

The brother nodded greedily as he fondled the capsule, too excited to care about the burning sensation he felt on his hands. It only provided further proof of this divine gift. It was a sign from the heavens, he happily thought as he followed his swirling flow of logic: blue was water and water was life and life was hope.

And if anyone needed hope in a capsule, it was this dead-end town. Whatever that magical substance was, soon he and the town would not feel trapped and abandoned anymore. Good fortune was only seconds away.

"Thirty bucks for the capsule," the owner's brother nodded as he took out his wallet. "Final offer. You ain't gonna get much more than that around these parts, anyways. It's all I got and I don't think my brother's gonna spring for something like that."

The price was right and the deal was sealed. The young men nodded, one of the two grabbed the cash, they thanked the man and left with their wheelbarrow. The day was a productive one and almost worth the burns on their hands. It was off to another scrap yard to sell the rest of the metal from the morning's haul.

The newly-minted owner of the Godblaze curiosity smiled as he stared lovingly at the capsule's magical window. "Think I'm gonna make the wife a ring with this stuff. Just have to figure out a way of opening it."

"I'm sure she'll love it," nodded the owner's wife in begrudging, and sudden envious agreement. Whatever his brother wanted to use it for, it didn't matter, so long as he was willing to share the godly light with the rest of the family. That's all that mattered.

V

Godblaze. What a beautiful way to bless the desperate, thought the junkyard owner's brother as he finally cracked open the capsule and marveled at the brilliant azure dust inside. Sticking his index finger in the open capsule, the man took out a small amount of the powder and used it to make a cross on his hand.

Taking his wife's wedding ring, the man dipped it in the capsule, then carefully took it out. The wondrous blue hues were just what the dented ring needed. Whatever problems were in their marriage would soon disappear. The blue fire would guarantee it.

The possibilities were endless – or would end as soon as the Godblaze ran out. That thought made the man uneasy. This had to be doled out very carefully – first to his family, then to those who truly deserved it, providing there was any left over.

So far, he and his wife were covered. That was good. Now it was time for the children to get their dose of divine glitter. He called his brood of eight -- no child older than ten – to come for a special treat. Slowly, noisily and clumsily, the children eventually came over and laughed with delight as their father showed them the shining Godblaze, and told them to decorate themselves with it.

"Make a wish when you do it; God listens to you when you're in the blue fire," he told them with paternal confidence. The children happily obeyed their father's advice as they bathed in the Godblaze. Giggling, running, and yelling, they all began to glow as they rubbed the Godblaze on their faces, hands, and bellies. Some of the older children prayed as they ritualistically applied the dust to their bodies; the eldest daughter drew a circle in the center of the room with the Godblaze, and then lay down in the middle.

The blissful scene was interrupted by a knock on the door. Somewhat vexed, the man got up and opened the door. It was his brother.

"What?"

"See you've been dipping into the holy powder," his brother muttered, staring at his brother's glowing hands.

"I bought it; I can do whatever I want with it," his sibling snapped defensively as he anticipated his brother's impending request.

"Just remember I hired you when you couldn't get a job to support all your kids and that woman you married. I want some of it."

"I don't have much left."

"I don't need much, just enough to ensure I'll still have a job for you tomorrow when you come in to work. Business hasn't been too good lately. I need some of that Godblaze."

"I thought you didn't believe in that stuff."

"Business is getting worse by the second. Do I get some? Does the Godblaze work if you don't share it with your family? Could be trouble – you wouldn't want to make God mad or anything, do ya?"

Angrily, his brother stomped into the living room to retrieve a miniscule amount of Godblaze. Putting the powder in a small plastic bag, he gave the dust to his brother.

"Don't let the word get around. That's it. I won't have any more for you."

"See you tomorrow at work. And God bless you, brother."

No sooner had the man closed the door, another loud knock came from the same direction. Reluctantly, he turned around and opened the door.

A distraught woman, no younger than forty, was standing before him.

She made no attempt at introducing herself to him. "Mister! Mister! I heard you have the magic powder from God. My poor old mother is dying of cancer. We need some of that stuff to cure her. I saw you give some to that guy. Give it to me, mister! I need the magic powder."

The Godblaze secret was officially out.

VI

"We got problems," the old man spat as he moved in closer to the young scavenger who sold the Godblaze two weeks ago.

"What are you talking about?"

"They're fighting for it," the older man replied sternly as he stared angrily at his grandson.

"Who's 'they'? What are they fighting about?"

"The Godblaze. The stuff you sold to that guy at the scrap yard. They say it was you and your friend who found it. There isn't enough to go around, and everybody wants the shiny blue. They want to bathe themselves and their children in the light of the heavens and be blessed. Word got out and now there's screaming and fighting in the streets. People are getting mugged for that powder."

"For God's sake, can't they learn to share?" the young man's partner snapped angrily as he tried to massage his sore shoulder. The hard labor of his work was quickly taking a toll on his body, and his temper had become short and severe.

His friend interjected. "I have a better question: Why do they have to take a goddamn shower in it in the first place? I don't understand why they all lost their heads over this glowing crap. It doesn't do anything. It's just some stupid powder."

"Because you sold it to them as a miracle light," the older man spat. "They need hope. You gave it to them with that Godblaze. They're tired of working like slaves and making themselves so old and sick. They want God to solve their problems and the Lord knows they've got plenty of those. All of them in this town. No one wants to be left behind here when the *good* luck comes."

"Well, they can't all have it at this rate, can they? Who knows what that stuff is, anyway. You don't see me taking a bath in it."

"But the children do."

"There wasn't that much in there. How could they still be using it?"

"They don't need a lot to get the glow. I'm sure it's run out. At least, that's what the guy who bought it from you says. I think he's for real this time. People are threatening to burn his house down for the Godblaze. He's terrified. It's brought nothing but bad luck to this town."

"People just going crazy. It'll die down. No bad luck about it."

"I think there is," the old man continued as he glared at the two dismissive young men. "People are fighting and screaming now. They never did before. I think whatever it was, it got God angry at us. You'll see. It'll get worse."

The scavengers just rolled their eyes, grabbed their tools and left for their daily hunt, leaving the old man, enraged and desperate.

"I heard what you told them," a female voice shouted as the startled man turned around. "I think you're right about bad things happening."

It was the junkyard owner's wife.

"The fighting?"

"More. Everyone in my family's gotten sick – my husband, my kids, me. I thought {it was} it was something we ate, but then other people got sick and they didn't eat what we did."

"Godblaze people?"

"Every one of them."

"I knew it. God's punishing us for fighting over his miracle. If people could only learn to share God's blessings…"

The woman felt too sick to argue with the old man. Whatever this illness was, it was making everyone sick in short order. But, why would God punish innocent children and their selfish parents alike? Why were those who asked for the Godblaze for altruistic reasons as afflicted as those who wanted it to ensure that they won the lottery? No, this wasn't God.

It was the Godblaze. It could be nothing else. Even now, no one knew what the mysterious substance was. They only knew where it came from, if the scavengers were to be believed.

Running toward her brother-in-law's house, the woman knocked on the door and was led inside by the man's ill wife. The sickly woman made no objections when her sister-in-law took the capsule and what little was left of the Godblaze, placed it in a bag, then took the package and left for the bus stop. She would go to the hospital – someone there would have to know if this strange blue dust really was the reason everyone in town suddenly fell ill. The scavengers said they found the mystery powder at the demolished cancer clinic – and it was time to find out what it was used for.

VII

"Cesium-137! My god. I still can't believe it. Do you understand what that means?"

"It means disaster on an epic scale. This is radiation, pure and simple. Anyone who's been exposed to this powder has been poisoned. They'll be lucky if they don't die. How many people were in contact with this?"

"The woman who brought it to the hospital said most of her neighborhood had some sort of contact with it. Children rolled around in it. Some of them even ate it for good luck – or to get closer to God. We'll have to send a team to examine both the people and infrastructure there – tear down anything that's been contaminated and treat the sick. Obviously, everyone on that bus she took and the hospital is going to have to be tested for radiation poisoning. If any out-of-towners got in contact with it, they'll have to be tracked down. What a mess!"

"How's the girl?"

"In critical condition and she's going downhill fast. They don't think she'll make it. Some of the others aren't in much better shape."

"Why the hell wasn't the cesium removed from that clinic in the first place?"

"That's for the investigators and police to find out. The scavengers who found the device sold the parts to several scrap yards; so tracking down all the contaminated metal is going to be hard work."

"This is a nightmare."

"It's only the beginning. I have to send in a report by tonight. The press is all over this, too."

"And the radiation is all over town. Right now, everyone in that city is in danger. I'd rather take my chances with the reporters than the cesium."

VIII

Another morning and another day for scrounging and searching for scrap metal. The going had been nearly impossible – so much of the junk metal had been removed from town, the one-armed scavenger pondered as he followed his taller partner to a newly abandoned warehouse. The signs of Cesium-137 were everywhere. The already dilapidated homes were torn down. The junkyards were razed to the ground and left barren. There were far fewer people in the neighborhoods – there were few children in town, most having succumbed to the effects of the Godblaze. People were missing hair and body parts. The young scavenger himself has lost his own limb at the shoulder after handling the ill-fated canister.

Everything seemed to both come to a standstill and radically change since the effects of the Godblaze became public knowledge. Police, doctors, reporters, and the government were involved, all asking question after question. With each death, more questions had been asked: when the first child died, the questions were angry and shrill, but by the time the junkyard owner's wife perished, the questions had become clinical and routine. But, for all the questions asked in those painful months, few answers were ever found. No one was truly held accountable, and no one in town knew whom to turn to or who to trust.

With that thought on his mind and an empty sack in his remaining hand, the young scavenger forced himself to stand up straight, and then cocked his head back and briskly walked inside the empty building, ahead of his partner who, at least, still had most of his arm intact. There was still one pair of arms between them, and they had to use whatever remaining resources they had to the best of their ability.

The wind felt cold and damp. It was too dark to see very much around, yet there was no other choice: they had to go out to-

271

morrow. They had to go forward tomorrow. They had to go searching tomorrow. They had to go on tomorrow.

They had to go, survive, push, and hunt until they found what they were looking for.